KILLED IN CORNWALL

JANIE BOLITHO

Allison & Busby Limited
12 Fitzroy Mews
London W1T 6DW
www.allisonandbusby.com

First published in Great Britain by Allison & Busby in 2002.
This paperback edition published by Allison & Busby in 2012.

A CIP catalogue record for this book is available from the British Library.

10 9 8 7 6 5 4 3 2 1

ISBN 978-0-7490-1163-5

For Jim Parsons;
my husband, friend, support and critic!

CHAPTER ONE

With thick grey hair cropped straight at chin level and a dark blue skirt and cotton blouse encasing her solid frame, Doreen Clarke might have been sixty rather than almost a decade younger. 'I'm off now, Cyril,' she called from the kitchen door of her bungalow in Hayle, her voice more quietly pitched than usual. 'I'm meeting Rose for coffee before I do the shopping.'

Cyril looked up from the tomato plants he was pinching out. Since he had been made redundant from the mine, several years before the very last one had ceased to operate, plants and vegetables had become his obsession. No longer able to dig tin out of the ground, he now spent most daylight hours tending things he had put into it.

'Give her my best then.' He studied his wife's tear-stained face. 'Don't take on, love. It had to 'appen at some point and she was over seventy.'

'I know. I'll be all right. It's just that I'll miss her.' Doreen blew her nose and stood taller, hating her weakness to show. 'I'll see you later.'

Cyril frowned. There must be something he could send over to Rose Trevelyan. The strawberries weren't quite ripe yet, it was too soon to pull radishes and it would be another week or so before the runner beans were ready for picking. 'I'll just cut a few of these for her.' He indicated the old-fashioned roses with their heady scent which the hybrid, disease-resistant varieties lacked. Well-oiled secateurs snipped ten long thorny stems from the bush. Their pinkish white buds were already fragrant and insect free; any aphids were squeezed between Cyril's thumb and forefinger on a daily basis. He handed them to Doreen who placed them lengthways in her wicker shopping basket.

'I'll see she gets 'em,' she said as she squinted over her husband's head. The first two weeks of June had been scorching, no hint of cloud in the arc of sky the colour of cornflowers. Now it was oyster grey with patches of mist rising from the Hayle estuary. 'I'll be back about one.' Doreen took her waterproof jacket from one of the hooks on the back of the kitchen door, twitched the net curtain at the window next to it then went out to her car and started the engine. She tried not to think about Phyllis Brown.

The weather worsened as she drove towards Penzance. Descending towards the dual carriageway, she saw the mist rolling landwards off the horizon, obliterating the wide curve of land on the far side of the bay until it finally obscured St Michael's Mount. She flicked the wipers to clear the windscreen of moisture.

It was Saturday. Every Saturday since she was a child she had gone to Penzance to shop. In those days she had ridden over with her mother on the bus and, if she had been good, was given sixpence for niceys, sweets she wasn't allowed to eat until the afternoon; sherbet lemons which, in the summer, stuck together in the white paper bag, halfpenny chews which blackened her teeth or a couple of ounces of butterscotch which the confectioner broke from a block with a hammer. They had been good days but hard work for her mother. Doreen had a small car which conveyed her to her various cleaning jobs and the supermarkets where she bought food she could put in the freezer. Gone were the days of scrag end of meat which simmered with vegetables for hours until it was rich and tender, days when she had also made her own bread. Since Cyril was made redundant she had had to go out to work herself and there wasn't the time, nor did she have the inclination to cook as she used to.

The weekend traffic was surprisingly light. It was too early for the long queues of late July and August. Doreen turned into the car park at the top end of Penzance. She bought a ticket, stuck it on the windscreen, locked the car then walked down Causewayhead to meet Rose. Only delivery vehicles were permitted to use the unpavemented road during business hours. Outside the shops on either side of the cobbled incline were displays of goods; hardware and ironmongery, flowers and plants and stalls of vegetables, brightly coloured and mounded high, organic or otherwise. Doreen ignored them. Coffee first, shopping later.

Rose was sitting at a table in Carwardine's, a cafetiere of strong Sumatran coffee in front of her. She smiled as Doreen, bundled up in her unsightly waterproof, her basket over her arm, approached her table.

"Tiz a real mizzle out there. Typical June

weather.' In her usual fashion she spoke without the preface of a greeting. It was as if she had so much to say that time would be wasted on such formalities.

Rose nodded. Mizzle. The word was more than local dialect, it had a distinct meaning; more than mist but not quite rain, a fine precipitation which penetrated clothes insidiously and was so typical of West Cornwall. But it did wonders for skin and hair.

The cafe was steamy and overwarm but it was still too early for it to be busy. 'What would you like?' the waitress asked once Doreen was settled in her chair.

'Tea for me, please, and a nice toasted teacake. These are for you,' she continued, dismissing the waitress and reaching into her basket for the flowers. 'My Cyril's real fond of you, not that he'd ever say so.'

'They're lovely. Please thank him for me.' Rose could picture him, wrapped up against the weather, the cap he always wore as a substitute for his miner's helmet perched firmly on his head, his gnarled, calloused hands ingrained with soil as he worked away in his garden where not an inch of ground was wasted. 'That reminds me, do you know anyone who'd be prepared to have a go at my garden? It'll only need a couple of sessions. The lawn really needs some sort of treatment and the trees at the back are so out of hand they're blocking the light.'

'It's a bit of heavy work you want then. Let me think.'

The waitress returned with a tray. Doreen poured her tea, added milk then blew on it. She took a sip, buttered her tea-cake and began to chew.

Rose's granite house was on the road between Newlyn and Mousehole. It stood on the top of a steep drive. With no buildings on the opposite side of the road she had an uninterrupted view of the whole of Mount's Bay. The main garden was at the side. It had been levelled atop a brick and earth wall. A narrow path ran from the drive around to the front where a few shrubs flourished and a small wall was the only protection from a drop down into the road. Behind the house, between it and a granite cliff, grew a tangle of brambles over which towered two trees and an evergreen which had never stopped growing. To clear it would take proper equipment and someone who knew how to use it. Doreen, who seemed to know everyone in West Penwith, was bound to come up with a suitable person.

'Dave Fox, that's your man,' she said with a decisive nod which caused crumbs to fall from her lower lip. She brushed them from her skirt.

Rose poured more coffee and stirred it. Dave, not David. David had been her husband's name, the man she had met soon after coming to Cornwall straight from Art College. They had enjoyed over twenty happy years of marriage, a marriage which was childless although they never knew why, unless the illness which had finally killed David was in some way responsible. Rose had done her grieving. Those first two years were the hardest of her life. There were still moments when shadows of that grief took her unawares and tears would fill her eyes, but they were, at last, becoming fewer. 'Do you have his telephone number?'

'Not on me, but I can let you have it. He can turn his hand to most things, can Dave. He's been working for the Petersons, where I go on Wednesdays. They're not bad, not for newcomers, and they pay well.'

High praise indeed, Rose thought. To Doreen, newcomers were alien. Anyone who had crossed the Tamar Bridge to live in Cornwall was not to be trusted for at least ten years. But the mines had all closed, the government was doing its utmost to put an end to fishing and farmers were under the cosh. Only tourism was left. Many youngsters had to move away to find work and the houses they would have lived in were sold at over-inflated prices to those who could afford them. Rose regretted the changing way of life. 'Sorry, Doreen, I was miles away. Is something the matter?' Only then did she see that her friend was upset.

'It's Phyllis, Phyllis Brown. I heard this morning that she died last night.'

'Oh, Doreen, I'm so sorry.' She reached across the table and patted her plump hand.

'I expect it was a release for her, she'd been ill a long time.'

'What'll Nathan do?'

'I've no idea. His aunt's with him at the moment. I felt I should go and see 'en but I didn't like to intrude too soon.'

Rose had met Phyllis several times, before and after she was bedridden, but Nathan, the son, she had only seen on two occasions. He was an unexpected child, born illegitimately when Phyllis was thirty-six. No one but Phyllis knew who the father was.

Doreen shook her head. 'He was devoted to her, heaven knows how he'll cope on his own.

He can cook and that, but it's just that she was always there.'

Rose didn't know what to say. She had known men like Nathan, men who stayed at home with their mothers out of duty or pity or fear, men who had sacrificed their own happiness until it was too late to know how to find it. She poured the last half cup of coffee aware of how much Doreen would miss Phyllis. Despite her many cleaning jobs Doreen always had time for her friends. 'If there's anything I can do, just ask.'

'There is something. Would you come to the funeral with me? Cyril didn't really know her and he's got a thing about funerals lately. Probably reminds him of his own mortality.'

Rose sipped the last of her coffee. She felt tired. It had been a long week and there was a longer one to follow, culminating in an exhibition in Bristol. 'Of course I'll come. Just let me know when it is.'

Doreen nodded. 'Here, you'd better have this for the flowers.' She handed Rose a plastic carrier bag. 'Wrap it round the stems and tie it or you'll prick yourself.'

Rose, used to her friend's non-sequiturs, did so. 'Please thank him for me.'

'I will. Now, where's my list? Cyril wants

me to get 'im some of that new denture stuff he saw advertised on TV. He's a real mug for they adverts, he believes everything they say, does Cyril. Still, if it keeps 'en happy. Got much to do yourself, maid?'

'A couple of bits and pieces then I'm getting my hair cut.'

'Not short, I hope?' Doreen looked horrified. Rose's naturally wavy auburn hair hung to her shoulders. That morning it was held back in a wooden clasp. A few tendrils, made wavier by the moisture-laden atmosphere, curled around her neck. Although Doreen dressed and acted as though she were a refugee from the 1950s, she recognised Rose's attractiveness. She was small-boned and dainty, with youthful movements and a pretty face but it upset Doreen that she mostly wore jeans or a denim skirt when she would look lovely in a nice frock.

'No, just the ends trimmed.' Rose tried not to smile. Doreen, only eighteen months older than herself, had a tendency to mother her.

'Well, I'd best be off, too. 'Tis my turn to pay.'

'Thank you.' Doreen was not well off but she had pride. Rose respected that. She picked up the roses and the bag containing the books she would change on the way home now that the library stayed open on Saturday afternoons.

Doreen tutted. 'All that reading. It can't be good for your eyes. Give me the telly any day.'

Rose hid a smile. Doreen had an irrational fear of microwaves – she said she was sure they would give you radiation sickness – but some modern technology, it seemed, was perfectly acceptable.

'I'll give you a ring with that number,' Doreen promised as she zipped up her jacket and went to the desk to pay.

They walked to the end of Causewayhead together. The mizzle had eased and patches of blue sky were appearing between clouds. They crossed to the Greenmarket. Doreen said goodbye and walked along towards the local chemist's, Rose went to the greengrocer's. Her appointment was not until eleven forty five. She stood gazing at the huge array of summer fruit and vegetables displayed on the pavement outside Tregenza's and was, as always, tempted to buy more than she needed. From the baker's on the other side of the road came the appetising smell of pasties and newly baked bread. Greengrocer's and pasty shops, Penzance had more than its share of both.

Having finished her shopping Rose walked down The Terrace in Market Jew Street. Curved steps with metal rails led down to the road which ran steeply down the sea. Fingers of watery sunlight now rippled on its surface and small boats could be seen in the distance.

For the next hour Rose sat impatiently whilst her hair was washed and trimmed and blow dried, a ritual which took place only twice a year. She had never been able to understand women who went regularly and actually enjoyed the experience.

The girl attending to her had given up trying to make small talk and got on with the job. Rose was grateful and tried to think about work.

Once, photography had been her mainstay, now she rarely took personal commissions although she continued to produce colour prints for Barry Rowe, a man she had known for almost three decades. He turned them into postcards. Barry owned a shop in the town which sold these postcards along with greetings cards, maps and souvenirs, all produced by local artists. Rose also painted small watercolours which were reproduced as notelets and cards left blank for personal messages. Wild flowers, woodland scenes, a disused mine stack or engine house standing out against the rugged Cornish scenery, these were subjects which sold well. But her main work now was in oils, dramatic work, capturing wild, winter seas or the treacherous coastline. She had even ventured into portraits and had never been more satisfied.

Geoff Carter, a local gallery owner, had staged her first one-woman show and now she was to co-host another in Bristol where she would be one of five artists. Twelve paintings had been required. Rose had worked very hard to produce them and was now in the process of choosing frames. This was the hardest part; framing could make or break an oil.

She sighed. On top of that was the class she took on Wednesday evenings and for which she had to prepare. This was another of Geoff Carter's ideas. He had persuaded Rose to take the overflow from another tutor who also used the annexe to his gallery for this purpose. To her surprise Rose enjoyed passing on her technique and skills although talent was a different matter since few of the students possessed much of it. But the classes had been a success and this was her third term.

'There you are, Mrs Trevelyan.' The girl held a mirror behind Rose's head. She glanced at the image reflected in the mirrored wall in front of her and nodded. Good, she didn't look any different. 'Thank you.' She handed the girl a tip, wrote out a cheque and left.

The sky had brightened further. There was no longer any dampness in the air and the warmth of the sun could be felt once more. St Michael's Mount was visible again, starkly rising out of a cobalt sea, the castle, the home of Lord St Leven, seemingly balanced atop an almost triangular rock. Rose stood looking at the view, drawn, as always, by the indescribable colours which had brought so many artists to the area over the years. It was the narrowness of the peninsula, surrounded by water, which caused the quirks of light, the startling clearness of the air, the shades of blues and greens which seemed impossibly unreal unless you were there to witness them for yourself.

She retraced her steps, her calf muscles working hard as she walked back up Market Jew Street. Crossing the road she turned left, passing the Acorn theatre which was housed in an old chapel, before she turned left again and bypassed the sub-tropical gardens where succulent plants with enormous flowers towered over her. She continued on through the narrow lanes lined with pretty cottages or Georgian houses until she came to the library. She handed over her books, chose four more, then made her way down Morrab Road to the Promenade.

A group of boys skate-boarded along its wide surface and used the steps of the shelters to attempt manoeuvres none of them were able to complete. Their wheels clattered in her wake. There were several dog walkers, a few elderly couples taking a stroll and a smattering of tourists enjoying a holiday before the schools broke up and accommodation would be hard to come by. Many local working women would be shopping or doing their housework on Saturday afternoon. How lucky I am, Rose thought, I can work whenever I want.

Ahead was Newlyn harbour. The masts and upright beams of fishing-boats loomed above the harbour walls like teepees stripped of their hide. Behind them the houses sloped up in tiers. She reached the end of the Promenade, descended the steps to the beach then joined the narrow path which would take her to Newlyn. To her left was the brilliant blue sea; to her right Bolitho Gardens where the fronds of the palm trees tapped in the gentle breeze. With the sun shining overhead she might have been in France or Spain.

Rounding the corner by the Newlyn Art Gallery, she thought about what Doreen had told her and the repercussions Phyllis's death would have for Nathan. Rose was not sure whether the house was rented or privately owned, neither was she sure what Nathan did for a living. Probably nothing, she realised. Someone had had to be at home on a full time basis to look after Phyllis.

Her books and shopping were becoming heavy. Rose would be glad to be home. She had given herself the day off – after a hectic week she deserved it. On Monday her paintings would go to the framers where she would negotiate a price, then she would scout around for post-card scenes. It was also time to plan her next watercolours. They would become part of Barry's stock next year as this season's cards had already been printed at his works in Camborne.

Halfway up the hill she stopped for a rest. Placing her bags on the ground she leant on the railings and looked down over Newlyn Harbour. Below, stretched in a short line on some rubber tyres strung together and floating in the water, half a dozen cormorants stretched their wings like Las Vegas showgirls in feathered costumes. The afternoon stretched ahead of her, as did the evening. Laura Penfold, married to a fisherman and Rose's best friend, had declined an invitation to supper because Trevor had landed that morning and they were going out for a meal. Lazy, idle solitude, Rose decided. Food and wine and a book. A treat. She picked up the bags and continued walking.

By the time she reached the top of the drive her fingers were red where the handles of the plastic bags had dug into them. With relief she unlocked the kitchen door at the side of the house and stepped inside. She plugged in the kettle, unpacked the shopping and hung some washing on the line strung between a tree and the shed. She had put it in the machine before she went out that morning. Nothing smelt nicer than cotton sheets which had dried outside in the salty sea air.

She made a mug of tea, picked up an apple and one of the library books she had chosen that morning then went outside to sit on the wrought-iron garden bench.

An hour later she was half dozing in the increasing heat of the sun when the telephone disturbed her. Rose went to answer it.

'I thought I'd ring before I forgot. My memory's like a sieve these days.'

Doreen, of course. Face to face or over the phone she still began without preamble. Even when leaving a message on the answering-machine no introduction was given. 'I've got Dave Fox's number. The gardener. It's a mobile.'

Rose jotted it down. 'Thanks, Doreen. I'll ring

him straight away. Did you thank Cyril for the roses?'

'I did. He said . . .'

'Sorry, I can't hear you.' One of the helicopters which serviced the Isles of Scilly was flying overhead. Rose could actually see the pilot.

'Must go. Cyril's waving to me through the window. Why he can't come in to speak to me, I don't know. Bye, Rose.'

He dare not come in, Rose thought, not if he's got muddy boots. The cleanliness of Doreen's kitchen floor was a matter of great pride. It was odd, she was equally as houseproud of her own bungalow as of the large properties she cleaned. It was beyond Rose to whom housework was something to be endured as infrequently as possible.

She picked up the phone again and dialled Dave Fox's number. It was a long time before he answered. Having given her name Rose explained what she wanted doing. 'Do you have the necessary equipment? I've only got basic tools.'

He said that he did and that he could come on Tuesday if that was convenient. 'I charge by the hour, by the way.' He named the price.

'That's fine, and Tuesday suits me.'

'I'll be there between nine and nine-thirty.'

'Do you know how to get here?'

'I'll find it.'

Rose went back to the garden. Dozens of small, white-sailed yachts had appeared. Some sort of race was in progress. A rowing-boat with an outboard motor chugged past, a lone man on board standing at the tiller. The engine spluttered and black fumes belched from the stern before it resumed its steady course across the bay towards Mousehole. Overhead seagulls swooped. Rose was oblivious to their noisy calls which were part of coastal living. She was wondering what sort of man Dave Fox was. He was well-spoken with the faintest hint of an accent she couldn't place. A newcomer? If so he had managed to impress Doreen Clarke. Rose had often been told that her curiosity went even deeper than the innate need to know possessed by the Cornish.

Well, I'll find out on Tuesday, she realised as she picked up her book and began to read.

By the fourth chapter she found she was thinking of Nathan Brown rather than the plot in which another son was motherless. It was always assumed that women were the carers, the ones who devoted their lives to a parent or spouse, but Rose was aware that many men also did so, men like Nathan, who had a gentleness about him, a gentleness hidden beneath a gruff exterior. Rose had never been able to decide whether this was due to a natural reserve, whether he had been cowed by an overbearing mother or whether, simply, like Trevor Penfold, he did not believe in wasting words. She hoped his future would be a happy one once he had done his grieving.

CHAPTER TWO

'I don't like to bother you on a Sunday, Rose, but you didn't get back to me and I need to know when I can collect the oils.'

'Oh, Geoff, I'm sorry. I completely forgot. I'm taking them to the framer first thing tomorrow and he promised they'd be ready by Wednesday morning. Can you pick them up from there?' Rose stood in the bay window. The brilliant sunrise, reflected in pink streaks across the water, had been no indication of the weather to come. The sky was now a pearly grey.

'Yes. No trouble. We're all set to go. I'll drive straight up to Bristol once I've got them. Why don't I drive you up as well?'

'The opening night isn't until Friday.'

'I'm fully aware of that, Rose, dear. I thought we could make a bit of a holiday out of it. You know, take in the theatre, go to the zoo.'

Nice try, she thought. 'Thanks for the offer, Geoff, but I'm up to my eyes this week.' Geoff Carter had been good for her career and she liked him, but no more than that; she enjoyed his company and appreciated the opportunities he had provided for her. He had taken her out to dinner a couple of times but on the first occasion, talking about his past and the times he had been unfaithful to his wife before she had divorced him, he had made it clear what sort of man he was. Good looking, yes: tall and lean, greying hair worn longish over the collar of his checked shirts; laughing eyes and a quirky, come-to-bed smile, but not the material for a relationship that was destined to endure for very long. He had apparently lived up to that smile and was not ashamed to admit it. Tempted, but only briefly, Rose was glad she had acted upon instinct and walked away. Had she become one of his conquests she would undoubtedly have lost his friendship, possibly his patronage and almost certainly the use of his studio annexe.

Geoff would transport her paintings in his

van which, with its wooden slats fixed against the panels in the back, was especially equipped to carry such work, whether oils with their heavy frames or watercolours and pastels fronted with glass. She knew they would arrive at their destination safely.

Rose was ironing, the radio tuned to a classical music station when Laura's thin body flitted past the kitchen window and appeared in the open doorway. The threatened rain had not fallen and the air was humid. 'Any chance of a coffee? Trevor's made of tougher stuff than me, he's gone down to do something to the engine of the boat before he takes himself off to the pub. Me, well, I'm feeling a bit fragile.'

Rose stood the iron on its end and laughed. 'I can see you're hungover, dear. I don't know what it feels like from inside but from here it's not a pretty sight.'

'Oh, some friend you are. I came here for sympathy and understanding, not a lecture from a hypocrite.'

'Stick the filter machine on, I've nearly finished.' There were only two pillowcases left in the basket. Rose shook her head. Laura; mother of three boys and a grandmother several times over. With her near black corkscrew curls trailing down her back, her skinny legs in harlequin patterned leggings topped by a long pink T-shirt, it seemed hard to believe she was fifty. And she was always so full of life, or, maybe, nervous energy.

Rose had met Laura within a month of coming to Cornwall. They had both been twenty-one then but now it felt as though they had known one another since birth.

Once the water began to gurgle through the coffee grounds, Laura sat down. 'For someone who claims to hate housework, you're very particular about your whites.'

'Ironing, I don't mind.' Polyester and mixed fibres might be easier to care for but it was a luxury to sleep between pure white Egyptian cotton sheets.

'What's new? Tell me the latest gossip, distract me from the effects of over-indulgence.'

Rose slid her hand inside a pillowcase in order to iron the flap. 'Geoff Carter asked me to go up to Bristol with him on Wednesday.'

Laura raised a dark eyebrow. 'I see. And what did he have in mind, I wonder, when the opening night isn't until Friday? Don't answer, it's pretty obvious. Are you going?'

'Of course not.' Rose unplugged the iron

and stood it on the worktop, then she folded the ironing-board and placed it in what once had been the larder, a small room at the back of the kitchen. Now it housed the deep freeze, her painting equipment and an assortment of boots and coats. Instead of food, the marble shelves held bits and pieces that might one day be useful again.

She got out milk and sugar and poured the filtered coffee into two red mugs decorated with yellow tulips and green leaves. Six of them hung from hooks beneath open shelves upon which local pottery glazed in primary colours was arranged. 'Oh, and I've got a gardener coming on Tuesday.'

'Really? A touch of the Lady Chatterley? Be careful, my girl, there are far too many men in your life already.' Laura sipped the coffee, black today, with three sugars. 'Speaking of which, how are things between you and Jack at the moment?'

Jack. Detective Inspector Jack Pearce. A thorn in her side or a source of pleasure? She could never decide which. 'So many questions. God, even a hangover can't stop you.' But she considered the question. 'Normal, I would say. For us.' It was an on and off relationship which, despite Jack's insistence that he wanted more, seemed to suit them both. Yet it had hurt Rose terribly when he had told her he was seeing someone else. It hadn't lasted long, but long enough for Rose to realise that she didn't want to lose him altogether.

'You're so well suited, you know. You like the same things and think the same way.' She sighed. 'The trouble is you're both so damn obstinate.'

Laura was right but Jack refused to understand that what he called her nosiness arose out of genuine concern for people. Rose knew that Laura only wanted to see her settled again but she was afraid that after David, anyone else would be second best. 'He'd cramp my style.'

'Someone ought to. Still, you do seem to be one of those people others like to confide in. So what's the work situation?' When the three boys were younger Laura had been a full time housewife and now they had grown up and had children of their own she was enjoying her freedom. With Trevor's hours being so unpredictable she did not want to get a job because she would hardly ever see him when he landed. Despite never having had any sort of career of her own she was extremely proud of Rose's achievements.

'It's going to be a busy summer.' Rose explained the projects she had lined up.

'And I've got the family coming in August.

They seemed to have arranged their visits like a relay team, and without consulting me.'

Rose nodded. 'That's the only drawback of living here, everyone wants to come and stay.'

Laura squinted shortsightedly at the luminous digits on Rose's cooker. 'Trevor'll be in the pub by now. Why don't you walk down with me and have a drink. You deserve it after all that ironing.'

'Okay, I think I will. I'll get a jacket.' No forecaster could predict with any accuracy the weather in West Cornwall. It could, and did, change in seconds. Penzance might be shrouded in fog whilst St Ives was basking in sunshine, and it still looked as though it might rain.

Rose locked the door and they walked side by side down the hill to the harbour. The tide was out. Trawlers and beamers were moored alongside the quays and the lifeboat, with its distinguishable orange and blue colours, sat waiting for the next emergency. Rose often wondered how Laura could bear it knowing that Trevor was out there in mountainous seas in order to earn a living that was likely to be taken away from him by ludicrous legislation or even by drowning.

Laura pushed open the door of the Star. There was no sign of Trevor 'He's next door,' another fisherman told her.

Trevor was standing at the bar of the Swordfish with a drink in front of him. It was a long, narrow room with an unpolished wooden floor, a place where fishermen could drink without worrying about their boots on a carpet or fish scales on the furniture. The jukebox was playing, clearly audible even over the loud conversations. 'Hello, Rose, what would you like?'

'Dry white, please.'

He ordered the larger measure and a double gin and tonic for himself and his wife. Rose grinned. Trevor had been at sea for ten days, he was now making up for lost time. Along the bar in bowls were garlic-stuffed olives, cheese, peanuts and onions. A Sunday lunchtime tradition. Later, the landlord would produce sausages and quarters of roast potatoes.

Laura and Rose did most of the talking. Trevor was a taciturn man, speaking only when he had something worth saying. He was dressed in jeans and boots and a fisherman's shirt, as were many other customers. His wavy brown hair was shoulder-length and a tiny gold cross dangled from one ear. Except for Saturday nights, and not always then, no one dressed up.

The bar filled up. After a second drink Rose said she was leaving.

'We're not,' Laura said as she smiled at Trevor.

So much for her hangover, Rose thought. But Laura was right, I did deserve a break. She made her way back up the hill knowing she would do nothing other than read a few more chapters of her library book.

Settled in her chair by the window, Rose remembered Phyllis Brown's funeral and her promise to Doreen. If it turned out to be on Friday or Saturday she wouldn't be able to go. She picked up her book. Until Doreen rang that dilemma couldn't be faced.

Dave Fox was washing the soil from his hands in the small sink in the kitchen area. He didn't usually work on Sundays but because of the good growing weather he was behind. Intermittent rain and sunshine had come to the aid of nature, and people needed their lawns cut and their hedges trimmed. Come October, when growth slowed, the work would drop off and he would do odd jobs or decorating instead. It was a life he had come to love; no mortgage, no ties, fresh air and freedom. No social security hand-outs either. He was an independent man, a man who had given up much to become so.

The caravan was on a piece of wasteland

near St Erth. The land belonged to a farmer who had no use for it because it was not suitable for cultivation or livestock. Dave assumed he was holding on to it until he could sell it at a good profit. Meanwhile, in return for a nominal rent, the farmer had connected him up to the electricity supply. The caravan contained all the modern conveniences and was very comfortable.

Beside it was parked a medium sized van, mud-splattered but in good working condition. Inside it were stored his tools. He picked up a towel and dried his hands as the caravan door swung open. 'Hi,' he said, smiling.

'Hi, yourself.' Eva had been walking. Her face was flushed and her long, almost black hair seemed alive because the humidity had fluffed it out around her face and thickened the natural curl.

It had taken Dave a week or so to become used to sharing his home but now he wondered how he could have believed himself happy before Eva's arrival. He liked to think he had rescued her.

She was twenty-five, almost ten years younger than him, and beautiful, with gypsy-like looks which she chose to accentuate with hooped earrings and long, diaphanous skirts. He was not sure if she was aware of the effect she had upon men.

'Shall we eat?' he asked. Preparing her food gave him pleasure and she needed looking after.

'Yes. I'm starving.' She sat on the seat inside the small table with her back to the window which framed her head and shoulders and watched as he dished up the food he had prepared earlier that morning and had left to cook very slowly in the oven. His movements were neat, economical and suited to the compactness of the kitchen where all he required was within easy reach. The meals he cooked were simple but healthy; mainly meat or fish in the form of stews and casseroles with vegetables. There wasn't the room for complicated preparations. Eva followed his example. If she made a salad she would use the hedgerow leaves Dave had told her were safe to eat, along with more conventional ingredients. She had learnt that nasturtium seeds soaked in pickling vinegar were almost as good as capers, which were expensive. But although the wild ones outside the caravan were in full flower, the seeds had not yet ripened.

'I've picked up another job,' he told her, handing her a plate of lamb stew and locally grown spinach. 'I forgot to tell you yesterday. A

Mrs Trevelyan. She lives in Newlyn and Doreen told me she's an artist.' Dave sat down. Yes, he had forgotten to tell Eva because when he returned yesterday evening she had taken his mind off everything.

'Oh?' Eva speared a cube of tender lamb.

'Some clearance work and a lawn that needs seeing to, nothing permanent. I'm going there on Tuesday. It probably won't take more than a couple of visits.'

'Is she famous? I've never heard of her.'

Dave frowned, considering the question. 'No idea.' He paused. 'Have you thought any more about getting a job?' She had talked of it and although he could afford to keep her he didn't want her to become bored. St Erth station was an easy walk. From there she could catch a train in either direction, to Penzance or eastwards to Camborne and Redruth or even Truro. The branch line to St Ives also ran from there. And there were buses.

'I'll make some enquiries tomorrow, I really will.' The past few weeks had been a sort of holiday. Having Dave look after her had been like balm to her damaged ego and body. It was time to repay his kindness.

Dave nodded. She had gone with him to jobs

on several occasions but the novelty of that, or the alternative of being alone all day, would soon wear off.

Their plates were empty. Dave lay on a bunk, his hands clasped behind his head. A combination of fresh air and physical work was tiring, but in a satisfying way, and he had never been more healthy. The fresh air and walking seemed to be having the same effect upon Eva.

Eva washed the dishes then sat beside him and slipped a hand beneath his white T-shirt. Dave closed his eyes and thought of nothing but the touch of her fingers on his warm skin. Chance had brought her to him, he prayed it would not take her away. She was the sort of woman he had dreamt of in his more conventional days.

Once the school holidays began and tourists were plentiful, Barry Rowe opened the shop on Sundays. But on dull weekends when early visitors who had visited all the attractions wandered around aimlessly he could also pick up quite a bit of trade. I might as well open today, he decided as he glanced at the sky from his front room window. Below, in the street, a few early risers were already looking in shop windows.

Because he had to pay regular visits to the print

works in Camborne, where many of his goods were produced, he employed two part-timers in the shop. But just recently he had been let down on several occasions and had made the decision to take on one person on a full time basis. Also it was hard to get sixth-formers to turn up in the holidays when the beaches and surfing were more appealing than earning a few pounds. Only two applicants had responded to the advertisement he had placed in the *Cornishman*. He had interviewed them both on Friday and informed them of his decision on Saturday. He had known immediately who was the more suitable but he wanted to let the unsuccessful woman down lightly, allowing her to believe he had more people to see. She had come across as domineering and prone to bad temper. Barry was not always comfortable with women, he would not have known how to deal with her.

Daphne Hill had been his choice. She was a smartly dressed woman about his own age with two adult children who lived in Somerset from where the Hills had recently moved. She had a pleasant manner and a low-pitched voice with a trace of a West Country accent, although it wasn't Cornish.

At four o'clock the sky darkened and rain

began to fall. The few people in the street hurried for shelter in pubs or restaurants or made their way home. Barry decided he would do little more trade so he shut the shop and locked the door. Having turned the sign to closed he went out to the back, through the small store-room and opened the door which led to his flat. He locked this behind him and went upstairs. I'll read the paper, get something to eat and watch some TV, he decided, knowing that his life would seem dull and predictable to many. But he was contented; he had friends, friends who insisted he join them for meals or the cinema, outings, which, once he'd made up his mind to attend he always enjoyed. Work, of course, kept him busy, too. And there was Rose. He smiled. When Rose was around nothing was dull. Rose, his friend, but also the woman he had loved for years who would never be more than a friend. Rose, who had met David in his shop. It was Barry who had introduced them never imagining that they would be married less than a year later.

In habitual manner he thumbed his ill-fitting glasses up his nose, settled his thin, hunch-shouldered frame in an armchair which had moulded itself to his shape and picked up a Sunday newspaper.

He stared at the headlines without taking them in. Lately he had smartened himself up, bought some new clothes, but Rose was right, his flat was shabby and uncared for. It wasn't as if he couldn't be bothered because he only rented it – it was his, he owned the property, upstairs and down. The deeds were with his bank. The room was in shadow. All he could see through the salt-grimed windows was the frontage of the shops and their upstairs store-rooms opposite and a patch of sky. Now that summer had arrived he might redecorate. Maybe Rose would help him chose some new furniture. Of course she would, but he wished he was in a position to share it with her.

He flung the paper on the floor and paced the room trying to imagine how it would look with painted walls rather than patterned paper. A sunny yellow, he thought, or white. Something to reflect as much light as possible. He couldn't do much about the state of the windows. The window-cleaner did them once a week along with the plate glass ones which formed the shop front, but it was an endless battle against the salt-laden air, especially when the wind drove the rain and the spray straight off the sea.

We'll make a day of it, he decided, me and

Rosie, when she can spare the time. Paint and curtains and furniture. Feeling optimistic he picked up the paper and started the cryptic crossword.

'Aren't you meeting Lucy?' Joyce Jago asked, trying to keep the impatience from her voice. She had washed the Sunday lunchtime dishes and was drying her hands on a towel. Ivan had gone off to play golf, Joyce wanted nothing more than to spend a few hours on her own with her painting.

'No.'

Joyce sighed. 'What's the matter, Sam?' Her daughter seemed to have everything going for her: youth, health, looks and a stable home. I was such a plain teenager, Joyce thought, but I was a damn sight happier.

'Nothing's the matter.' Sam's face was averted, her long, dark hair fell forward, hiding it altogether.

'Have you fallen out with her?'

'I wish you'd stop asking me questions. No, we haven't fallen out, it's just that she's changed her mind.'

Probably going through a late adolescence like you, my darling, Joyce thought but would never have dreamt of saying. Samantha believes she's an adult, that she knows all there is to know about life and love and emotions. And I expect she thinks I'm totally past it now I'm almost forty.

Sam picked up the mug of tea she had made. 'I'm going to my room,' she said.

Then please don't play your music too loudly. Joyce smiled at herself. Many of the sentences she addressed to Sam were silently spoken these days. It was a phase, this sullen awkwardness, she understood that, but one which she hoped would not last long.

It had started to rain. Joyce made herself some tea then sat in the window of the large lounge where she could look down over the rooftops of the houses below, between which she just make out a triangle of sea. She picked up her sketchpad and began the homework Rose Trevelyan had set them at the end of their last class.

Detective Inspector Jack Pearce swore under his breath. Another two attempted break-ins on Saturday night. No entry gained to either property but should they catch the perpetrators there would be a charge of criminal damage. He ran a hand through his dark, springy hair. Petty crime, now prevalent, was so time-consuming. Whoever was responsible for the latest spate of burglaries and attempted burglaries was by no means professional but they were not entirely stupid either or surely they would have caught them by now.

He glanced at his watch. The face was plain, the numbers Arabic and the strap leather. It was comfortable on his muscular, olive-skinned arm and did not catch on the hairs like his old one with the expanding bracelet. It had once been his father's. It was just after four on a Sunday afternoon. Too late to do anything useful with the day, apart from which it was raining. He was tempted to telephone Rose but he knew she had a busy week ahead of her and probably needed some time to relax.

He pulled on his jacket and went out to the car. Driving back to Penzance from Camborne where he was based he decided he'd have a walk, something he rarely did voluntarily or unless Rose was with him. A walk, a couple of pints in the Alexandra, known to everyone as the Alex, where there might be some cricket on the television, then home. It would do him good to relax, too, to forget about work and all that went with it. It was a rare occasion when he could afford that luxury, unlike Barry Rowe who seemed totally at ease at all times.

He parked outside his ground floor flat in Morrab Road. It was a longish road leading up from the seafront to the town centre. Large houses lined it, many now converted to guest houses or the offices of professional people; a few, like Jack's, contained flats.

When the rain fell more heavily he almost changed his mind about going out, but he had been sat behind his desk for much of the week and fresh air was needed. Not a man who enjoyed drinking alone, he decided to give Barry a ring and see if he would join him.

'Love to, Jack,' Barry said when he answered the phone. 'I was only reading the paper.'

'Ah, well, good. See you in the Alex in about an hour?' Well, well, what a surprise. Jack had been expecting a refusal or a feeble excuse as to why Barry couldn't join him. He can be so damn lugubrious at times, he thought as he pulled on a raincoat, but that afternoon Barry had sounded quite positive.

He walked towards the sea, head down against the rain and wondered if he was crazy. But the wind in his face was exhilarating and the worries of work disappeared. Soaked but feeling better for the exercise, Jack met Barry as arranged and a couple of pints turned into four.

* * *

Even though it was over, Lucy Chandler kept her eyes closed. She was afraid to open them, afraid of what might follow. After ten minutes, juddering with cold and shock, she tried to get to her feet but couldn't. On all fours she moved towards a tree and used the trunk to lever herself up.

It was late, very late, and she had told her mother she would be home by ten in time for her father's weekly telephone call. Her mother would be annoyed, she didn't like speaking to Dad if she could avoid it.

A sound escaped her, a sound she did not recognise as coming from her own throat. It was a mixture of terror and disgust. She tasted bile a split second before she bent double and vomited. She wiped her mouth on her sleeve and knew she had to get home.

Sore and aching and filled with revulsion, she staggered towards the main road. Home, she thought, I must get home. It was only that one thought that ensured she did. Had she let her mind dwell upon what had happened she would have collapsed on the spot.

It was a wet Sunday night with few pedestrians and even fewer cars. No one stopped for her, no one asked if she was all right. Seeing her, dishevelled and swaying, a stranger would have mistaken her for a teenage drunk. It was almost midnight when she reached home. Lights were on in all the rooms. She had no idea how she had got there, only that somehow she must have walked. 'Mum.' It might have been a whisper or a shout.

At the third attempt she got her key in the door. 'Mum.'

Gwen Chandler stood in the hallway. Her hand flew to her mouth. 'My God. Oh, my God, Lucy, whatever's happened?'

Lucy Chandler fell over the doorstep and lay still on the floor.

CHAPTER THREE

Rose turned into the narrow street and parked, hoping that no other car would require access for a few minutes. She opened the boot where the oils, carefully wrapped in sacking, were stacked between wads of newspaper. A rough wooden door to her left opened and a man in faded brown overalls came out to help her unload. Little sun penetrated the back street building but it was brightly lit within by fluorescent tubes suspended from the ceiling. Benches and tables held an assortment of sharp tools and samples of frames in the form of corners of wood and plastic in various colours.

'No problem,' the framer told her when she

had stressed the importance of the paintings being ready by Wednesday. He liked Rose Trevelyan and found her unassuming, unlike some of the artists with whom he came into contact. No pretensions, no boastfulness because she happened to possess talent and certainly not a 'luvvie' like one or two he could mention. He stuck a pencil behind his ear and walked with her to the door.

'Geoff Carter's collecting them. About lunchtime, he said,' she added as she hurried out and around to the driver's side of the car because another vehicle had pulled up behind it, waiting for her to move.

Thank you, she said silently to whatever forces governed the weather. Warmth seeped into her body as she negotiated the small labyrinth of lanes until she reached the main road and the roundabout where she turned left and headed towards Land's End. Behind her was the reinforced bag which contained her camera equipment. After months of preparing for the exhibition, photography would make a nice change.

She was going to tour the villages and take some preliminary shots for next season's postcards: Sennen Cove, Porthcurno, Logan Rock and Lamorna on one trip, Porthleven,

Poldhu Point, Kynance Cove and the Lizard on another. Sometimes she went further afield because although tourists tended to want pictures of the area in which they were staying they also bought views of places they had been to visit. So Falmouth, Helford and its river, Gweek and Rosemullion Head and the old fishing village of Coverack were other popular scenes.

If the weather held, which was never a certainty, she might even get some shots Barry could use right away. The light and colours which drew artists to Cornwall might come across as unrealistic in a painting but it was said that the camera never lied. Rose laughed. It didn't used to, now it could. Technology could turn a photograph into anything you wanted it to be.

She arrived at Sennen under a clear azure sky. The various blues and greens of the sea which depended on its depth were of such brightness and purity it almost hurt her eyes to look at them. Purple patches denoted rocks below the surface. It was as if dyes had been added to enhance the natural beauty of the coastline. It was hot now, hot enough to deserve the acknowledgement that the climate was sub-tropical, allowing the palms and yuccas to flourish, to grow to great heights and flower every summer. And there were fleshy, black succulents and pink flowered echiums which reached towards the sun like giant phallic symbols. These things draw the tourists as well as the artists, Rose thought as she got out her camera bag, reminding herself the purpose of her visit was work, not day-dreaming. The summertime pictures she took would sell. You never saw postcards depicting a fishing village or beach half obscured by mist or rain with the granite cottages, sea and sky merging into one dour, grey landscape, nor did you see the obsolete mining communities with their closed shops and signs of poverty. Visitors turned a blind eye to such things even if they did visit a mine that had been turned into a museum. Cyril Clarke had been invited to the opening of the one from which he had been made redundant. 'Bloody theme park now. Good men died there,' was all he had said, refusing to go, refusing to discuss it further. He felt it was an insult to the generations of men who had spent their working lives below ground.

Let's get on with it, Rose told herself as she attached a wide-angle lens and headed for a high vantage point.

The weather held, but not the clarity. As the heat increased, so did the haze and the shimmer over the sea. The water was now more silver than sapphire, the occasional ripple flashed gold in the sun. She experimented with various lenses and hoped she had created some worthwhile effects.

Late in the afternoon, having taken in two other locations, she made her way home, her face tingling from the heat of the sun. She was aware there would be a few more freckles across her nose.

Having unloaded her gear she took three rolls of film up to the attic where a small section had been sectioned off and adapted as a dark-room. Later, when she had eaten, she would develop the films. Making the prints could wait until tomorrow. Dust had accumulated on the table where she worked at her watercolours and gull droppings were splattered over the north facing velox windows. Fortunately they swung open at an angle of 180 degrees so she was able to clean them herself.

She descended the backless, wooden steps from the attic then the carpeted stairs which led down to the hall. Meat tonight for a change, she decided. Many of her evening meals consisted of the fish which Trevor gave her or which she bought for next to nothing from one of the fish buyers she knew. With a glass of chilled wine to hand she began to prepare her evening meal.

When she had eaten she rang her parents who had retired from farming in Gloucestershire and had moved to a cottage in the Cotswolds where the large garden kept them both occupied. Evelyn and Arthur Forbes were in their early seventies but were active and fit and travelled a lot, which they were unable to do when they had the farm. But they were no longer young, Rose never forgot that.

'A gardener?' Arthur said in disbelief when Rose mentioned Dave Fox.

'Just to do the heavy work.'

'Fair enough. You've never been one for looking after it properly. I'll put you on to your mother.'

'Hello, darling. How are you?'

'Oh, I'm fine, Mum, but busy.'

'And how's Jack?'

'I haven't seen much of him lately.' Rose knew how much her mother liked him and how much she hoped they would become a couple, even marry.

'Well, give him my love when you do see him.'

'I will.'

They chatted for a few more minutes then Rose hung up. Pleasantly tired from the effects of fresh air and sunshine, she went to bed.

When she woke at six, narrow yellow bands of sunlight ran across the carpet from between the small gaps at the sides of the curtains. *Dave Fox will be here this morning,* was her first conscious thought. Pulling on her towelling robe, she went downstairs to make coffee and to smoke a cigarette, one of the few she allowed herself each day. By six forty-five she was in the dark-room making prints from the negatives. It was better to avoid working in the confined space beneath the eaves when the heat built up.

When she had finished, she showered and dressed and rewarded herself with another mug of strong coffee, taking it outside to drink. Ahead, the stark outline of the curving coastline was in contrast to the turquoise sweep of Mount's Bay and the blue sky, which was striated by a few wisps of cirrus cloud.

Rose was sitting on the bench writing a shopping list when she heard a vehicle slow on the road below. A plain white van turned into the drive and parked behind her Metro. At the wheel sat a tanned man who looked to be in his early thirties.

He got out and nodded at Rose who, for no logical reason, felt guilty to be found sitting in the garden. 'Mrs Trevelyan? I'm Dave Fox.' He held out his hand. Rose shook it. He had a firm grip and callused palms and was a good foot taller than her. 'Thank you for coming.'

'If you'd like to show me what needs doing I'll get going.'

There was no hesitation, no suggestion that tea or coffee was a requisite before he started the job. But as he came with Doreen's recommendation she had not supposed he was a time waster.

'The lawn, as you can see.' She gestured towards the small hummocks and the accumulation of moss. 'And the trees at the back.' She led the way up the side of the house. The tangle of undergrowth was topped by the trees, one of which was now in full leaf and whose branches obscured much of the light from the spare bedroom. 'I don't know how it survives with that cliff behind it. Will you be able to work in such a small space?'

'Yes, once the brambles are cleared. I'll start with the lawn. You'll have some bare patches for a while. If nature doesn't do the job it might need re-seeding later.' He returned to the van and opened the back. Inside was a petrol mower, a strimmer, an electric saw and various other tools of his trade.

'Will you need a power point? There's one in the shed. I've got an extension lead, too, if necessary.'

'Thanks, but I've got my own.'

'I've got some work to do. If you need me just shout. I'll be upstairs.'

He nodded again and turned his back, sizing up the lawn.

Not knowing what else to say, Rose left him to it and went inside. Up in the attic she sorted though some paperwork and filed and labelled the negatives she had developed the previous evening. It was some time before she realised what a chance she had taken. Dave Fox was a powerfully built man, one she had never set eyes on before. She was alone and she had left the kitchen door unlocked and, foolishly, she had left her shoulder-bag hanging over the back of a kitchen chair. Rose shrugged. Her instincts were usually sound. He had not said much but Dave's quiet, professional manner suggested that he was trustworthy, and Doreen certainly thought so. She hoped she was right.

An hour later she went back downstairs and watched the man in question. His arm muscles swelled as he tackled the lumps in the lawn which she had never been able to get rid of. Fair hair fell over his forehead and she could see a triangle of sweat on the back of his T-shirt. He's very good-looking, she thought, but without any real interest. He wasn't her type and he was too young. As if he had read her thoughts he turned to face her. Rose blushed. 'I was wondering if you'd like some coffee,' she said.

'Yes, please.'

'How do you like it?'

'White with two sugars, please.' He straightened up fully and stretched his back, not stiffly, just as a precaution. He wiped the sweat from his face with his forearm and sank the fork into the soil which, beneath the grass, was still damp from the rain, then went to sit on the garden bench.

Rose made the coffee feeling uncertain of what was expected of her. Never having had anyone work for her, she wasn't sure whether to join him, to invite him in to the kitchen or to leave him to drink it alone. Politeness overcame her indecision. 'If you're hot why don't you come in for a minute.' The sun had not yet penetrated the kitchen which faced south and was still cool.

He got up and walked towards her, his size blocking the light from the doorway momentarily. Rose could smell his fresh sweat and noticed how blue his eyes were, but a paler blue than Jack Pearce's which were a striking feature combined with his dark hair and swarthy Cornish looks. 'Have a seat,' she said.

He did so, pulling out one of the heavy wooden chairs without scraping it on the flagstone floor. Rose handed him a mug, pushed the sugar bowl towards him and sat down herself. For several minutes neither of them spoke. 'Have you always done this sort of work?' She was genuinely interested. Barry Rowe would have said she was damned nosy, Jack would have accused her of inflated curiosity had either of them been present, but she also felt a need to break the silence.

'No. Not always.' He sipped the coffee which was scalding hot.

'I see.' End of conversation, Rose thought. Cyril Clarke, Trevor Penfold and now Dave Fox. Three men with few words. Or maybe Dave was shy; shy with women, or maybe her especially.

'I believe you're an artist.'

The statement surprised her. 'Yes.'

'I draw a bit myself.'

Rose nodded. This was dangerous territory. Would he want to bring some of his work along for her to look at? And what could she say if it was awful?

'Birds mainly, pencil sketches, I try to capture their wing patterns. It's only a hobby.'

But the request didn't come, for which she was grateful. 'Did you have to come far?' she asked in case another awkward silence developed.

'No. I live near St Erth. I have a caravan there.'

Hence only a mobile phone number, Rose realised. She still couldn't make him out. He was well spoken, his voice accent-less apart from a hint of what? Not Cornish, certainly. She smiled. 'Do you know I've never slept in a caravan, not even on holiday. Don't you find it cramped?'

'No. You get used to it. Lack of space doesn't bother me, I'm not one for possessions and I'm out of doors for most of the day. They're cheap to run, too.'

'Do you live there alone?' She blushed again. 'Forgive me, that was rude. It's none of my business.'

He looked away, trying not to smile at her obvious discomfort. 'Not any more. I've got a girlfriend.'

'Oh. Well, good.' Keep your mouth shut, girl, Rose told herself. If he wants to tell you things he will.

'Thanks for the coffee.' Dave stood and pushed his chair back under the table as quietly as he had pulled it out. 'I'll go and finish the lawn.' In two strides he was at the kitchen door. He ducked under the lintel, picked up his spade and got back to work.

Rose went upstairs and picked up the prints which were now dry. In the sitting-room she studied them in detail. One or two were perfect, some were good, but not good enough and a couple she put straight in the bin. She reached for a book on wild flowers which was kept on one of the shelves set into the recesses on either side of the fireplace. Thumbing through it she checked which would be flowering in hedgerows at the moment. She made some notes then wondered what time Dave would knock off and if there would be time to do some outdoor work. He would presumably want paying for the hours he had put in that day so she couldn't leave until he had finished and she knew how much she owed him.

By the time she had tidied the attic and cleaned the windows it was almost half past one. She was hot from the exertion and needed fresh air.

'Mrs Trevelyan?'

His voice reached her as she was coming downstairs. Rose found him standing in the kitchen doorway. He had not stepped over the threshold. 'I've finished the lawn. I'll come back next week at the same time and start on the back, if that's convenient. I have another job to go on to this afternoon.'

'That's fine.' She peered around him. 'Goodness, it looks much better all ready. How much do I owe you?'

'Twenty-two pounds fifty.'

She went to get her purse. She had enough cash with which to pay him. So much casual work was cash in hand and five pounds an hour was by no means extortionate even if it was more than many people earned.

He pocketed the money, thanked her, then packed up and left. As the van disappeared she heard the telephone ringing and hurried inside to answer it. There was enough of the day left to make a few sketches. God, and I haven't even started to prepare for tomorrow's evening class, she remembered as she picked up the receiver.

'Hello, it's me.'

'Jack?'

'How many men do you know with such a sexy voice?' He laughed.

'Oh, you'd be surprised, Inspector Pearce. One of them has just driven away.'

'Oh?'

She ignored the implied question. 'Did you ring for any particular reason or isn't there enough crime to keep you occupied?'

Jack wasn't sure what to make of her bantering tone. Maybe some man had been there, paying her attention. At least she wasn't snapping at him; being 'teasy' as his mother would say. 'I've got a few hours off, I was thinking we could do something.'

This, Rose realised, was one of the reasons why their relationship would never progress. Accepted, Jack worked odd hours, but when he was free he expected her to drop everything and join him. She worked, too, but few people understood how important it was to her. Artists did not simply go off with a blank canvas and knock off a painting then laze around until inspiration struck again. 'I've got rather a lot on at the moment, Jack. And there's the exhibition on Friday.'

'I know. And I wish I could be there. I'm pretty busy too, this is the only time I can spare to see you this week. We're still trying to clear up these break-ins.'

Rose sighed. She had heard the pleading in his tone even though he had not meant it to show. They compromised. Jack would meet her at six and they would go out for a meal. That gave her an hour or so in which to work.

Minutes after she had replaced the receiver the phone rang again.

'The funeral's tomorrow afternoon. Two-thirty. Can you make it, Rose? It's such short notice because the minister's going away. Phyllis was one of his most regular attenders so he wants to conduct the service himself. I only found out myself last night.'

'Of course. Where is it?'

Doreen gave her directions to the church and Rose said she would pick her up just after two.

'I do appreciate it,' she said. 'Thank you.'

Rose was aware that Doreen would need the comfort of another friend when saying goodbye to Phyllis. Hopefully Nathan's aunt would be there for him.

Having telephoned a florist to arrange flowers she left the house just as she was, in what had become her uniform; denim skirt, a short-sleeved shirt and espadrilles. Her hair was held back with a bright yellow band. Over her shoulder hung the large leather bag in which were pencils and various sketch pads. At the bottom of the drive she crossed the road to the safety of the pavement and walked along the coast towards Mousehole.

The pavement had now been widened to include a cycle path which she had yet to see anyone use, and extra seats had been added from which to admire the spectacular view. The rickety wooden railings had also been replaced. There was a long drop down to the rocks. Cars passed in both directions as did the buses whose route lay between Penzance and the picturesque fishing village with its narrow streets and tiny cottages. Rose passed several pedestrians, none of whom she knew, but they either nodded or said hello.

Sitting on a bench, she studied the shrubs and the wild flowers which grew high in the hedge and spilt down towards the rocks which lay hidden from the road. Gulls circled overhead and a male chaffinch, with its distinctive colouring, sang in a nearby tree. After a few minutes she began to sketch a purple flowered vetch with its delicate stem and pinnate leaves.

By five o'clock the sun was behind her and she had filled three pages, a single stem to each: vetch, cow parsley and common cleavers. Satisfied, she began the walk home. It was hot, but not unbearably so. When she reached the house and let herself in, she could smell the sun-warmed flesh of her arms. She realised there was now only about half an hour in which to shower and change and be ready for Jack. She put on a yellow dress and brown leather sandals with a small heel. Her hair, freshly washed and quickly blow-dried, swung around her shoulders feeling thicker for the inch she had had trimmed from it.

Jack rapped on the kitchen window just as she had finished getting ready. David used to admire her ability to do so in minutes. She let Jack in noticing how tired he looked.

'Um, you smell nice,' he said as he bent to kiss her cheek.

'I should do, it's the perfume you bought me.' His dark, springy hair had also recently been washed, it was still damp at the roots. She smiled, taking comfort, as she often did, from his size, his warmth and his familiar odour – a combination of clean cotton, lemony after-shave and the scent of his skin.

'I thought we'd go to Fletcher's. Is that all right with you?'

'Great.' She had not heard his car. 'Did you drive?' Jack shook his head. 'Okay, I'm ready.'

They set off, walking side by side in silence, enjoying the summer evening. Rose was disappointed he hadn't noticed the effort she'd made. Her normal attire was far less formal. At least he'd noticed the perfume.

They strolled along the Promenade and stopped to look out to sea. Few people, whether local or holiday-makers, could resist doing so. The familiar large white shape of the Scillion, returning from its daily crossing to St Mary's, rounded the headland as it passed St Clement's island. A few small craft drifted in the bay and a number of children swam in the water.

The Promenade was unspoiled, no buildings marred its length or wide expanse. On the opposite side of the road was the sole amusement arcade on the front. Above it was Fletcher's restaurant. It was a large, ornate place with views of the sea. Most of the seating was arranged in high-backed booths where wooden benches ran either side of big, solid tables. The menu was American-based; burgers and ribs and barbecued chicken, with the addition of specials and salads.

'Wine or a cocktail?' Jack asked when they had been seated. He grinned. 'Both, knowing you.'

'Naturally. We're on foot, after all.' Rose picked up the menu.

Once their cocktails had arrived and they had placed their order, ribs for Jack and fish for Rose, Jack began to relax. 'These burglaries are driving us mad. Ten successful ones and five attempts now. We're sure it's the same person, or people, but can we pin them down?' Rose might be irritating at times, occasionally interfering and always a mystery to him, but he trusted her totally. Nothing he said would go any further.

'What sort of burglaries?'

'Private houses. It seems whoever's doing it studies the residents' habits. Some have been in daylight.'

'No fingerprints?'

'Oh, yes, at several locations, but they don't belong to anyone known to us.'

'One of those gangs then?'

'Possibly.' The area had been targeted by gangs of thieves or conmen from cities, as had several other rural areas. They would come down, work the area then go away again before their crimes could be detected. Jack shook his head. 'On the other hand, these jobs don't look like the work of professionals. Rose, I want you to promise me you'll lock your door from now on.' And now a young girl had been raped. A statement had been given to the press but Lucy Chandler's name had not been released. Even Rose could not be given that information. 'Have you read today's *Western Morning News*?'

'No, I didn't have time to buy it. Why?'

If she didn't know he wasn't going to mention it. 'It's nothing. Sorry, Rose, I shouldn't be burdening you with this, we're supposed to be enjoying ourselves. Tell me what you've been up to. No, wait,' he held up his hands in mock despair, 'I think I'd rather not know.'

'Well, that man I was telling you about on the phone, he's a gardener.' But was he just a gardener? Dave Fox would have plenty of opportunities to study people's movements. Was she being ridiculous? Rose wasn't certain but she'd heed Jack's warning.

'What? For your small patch? Your dad been on at you again, has he?' Jack liked Rose's parents as much as they liked him and he knew how much they loved and cared for their own garden.

Rose laughed. 'No. I wanted the lawn sorted out and you know how badly the back needs clearing.'

'I could've done it for you.'

She detected a hint of jealousy and his next words proved her right.

'What's he like?'

'He's big and strong and very handsome. He told me he lives in a caravan and that he hasn't always been a gardener. Apparently he's just got himself a new girlfriend. He's not local. I wonder if he's got a past, if this is his way of turning his back on it all?'

'Honestly, woman, I meant is he doing a good job? I should've known you'd subject him to an interrogation.'

She sniffed. 'He seems to be pretty efficient. Didn't you notice the lawn? It's flat now.'

'Maybe so, but Rose, you know what you're like. Don't go poking your nose in. The man's entitled to his private life.'

'Don't go poking your nose in,' she mimicked. 'Anyway, Doreen Clarke recommended him.'

'Then say no more.' The waitress placed the dry white wine and two glasses on the table. Jack thanked her, indicating that he would pour it himself. 'How is Doreen?' At the mention of her name Rose's smile had faded.

'She's just lost a very old friend.'

'I'm sorry. You knew her?'

'Phyllis? Yes, I did. Not well but I met her on several occasions. I'm going to the funeral tomorrow, Doreen asked me especially, although I would have gone anyway.'

Jack reached across the table and took her hand. All right, Rose might be trouble at times but she was always there for someone else's troubled times.

'There's a son. Nathan. He's about forty. Heaven knows what'll happen to him now.' She smiled ironically. 'It's my turn to apologise. As you said, we're supposed to be enjoying ourselves. And, as you can't have helped but noticed, Inspector Pearce, my glass is empty.'

Jack smiled back even though Lucy Chandler was still on his mind. She had spent the remainder of Sunday night in hospital, bruised and shaken but with no serious injuries. The damage to her mind might be a different matter.

Pale-faced and a little overweight, she had come across as sensible and reasonably coherent. Unfortunately, her attacker had approached her from behind and had raped her from behind, his hand over her nose and mouth.

'I didn't turn around, I couldn't,' she had told them. 'Even when I knew he had gone I stayed where I was and kept my eyes closed. I thought if he knew I'd seen him he'd come back and kill me.'

The equivalent of playing dead, Jack realised. It was often a victim's natural reaction.

'Jack? Are we leaving or are you falling asleep? Come on, you can walk me home.'

He smiled again. Surely that was an invitation to stay the night.

CHAPTER FOUR

By Wednesday morning Gwen Chandler needed to get out of the house. More than that, she needed someone to talk to, someone other than her daughter or the WPC who had been assigned to them for as long as they needed her. Nothing she had said so far had encouraged Lucy to talk.

Gwen could not begin to imagine the effect the rape might have on her daughter's future, she only knew what it had already done to herself. Her guilt was as predominant as her pity; a mother's guilt, which led her to believe she could somehow have prevented the events of Sunday evening if she had acted differently or brought Lucy up some other way. But Lucy, unlike her older brothers who had now left home, had never been easy to handle. I don't even know if she was a virgin, Gwen realised as she picked up her handbag. But Lucy had just had her seventeenth birthday and Gwen wasn't sure if it was any of her business. The boys had done well for themselves, like their absent father whom she had long since divorced. At one point she had wondered if Lucy was employable but she had found herself a job in a hairdresser's and seemed to enjoy the training.

'I'm going for a walk,' she told the two women who sat in silence in the living-room. 'I won't be long. Is there anything you want, Lucy?'

Lucy shook her head. It was as if her mother didn't exist. The bruises were healing, they had not been as bad as they appeared initially, but it was obvious the shock had not yet worn off. When she's over this, if she ever gets over it, we'll talk, Gwen decided. For now there was nothing she could do. Any attempt to touch Lucy had been brushed off. There seemed to be no way in which to comfort her. Alone with Jenny, the WPC, Lucy might feel less inhibited and therefore more inclined to talk.

She walked down from the house towards the sea. On the Promenade she punched out Laura

Penfold's number on her mobile phone, hoping that she would be at home. Unlike Gwen she didn't have a job, although Gwen had taken the week off from the building society where she worked. 'Hello, Laura,' she said with relief. 'I've got a problem, can you spare me a few minutes?'

'Of course I can. Where are you?' Laura heard traffic and the sound of the sea sucking at pebbles.

'Half way to your place.'

'Then come straight here.'

Laura waited, wondering what had caused her self-contained, capable friend to seek her advice. Since Gwen's husband had run off with someone else she had found full-time employment and kept the house and family together until the boys had left home. Only Lucy was left. Lucy then, Laura decided as she got out things for coffee in her cramped kitchen in the small, three-bedroomed fisherman's cottage where she and Trevor had somehow managed to bring up their own three children. It was in a back street with no view other than similar cottages that were, built in close proximity to withstand the winter gales and onslaughts from the sea before the stone barrier was put in place to try to contain it.

'You look dreadful,' Laura said when she

opened the door to let Gwen in. 'Come and sit down and have a coffee.'

'It's Lucy,' she began once Laura had handed her a cup of coffee. 'I just don't know what to do, Laura. I can't find the right things to say.' She shook her head as she realised her own stupidity. 'Of course, you don't know. How could you?' No one does except us and the police, and him, Gwen was thinking. She took a deep breath. 'She was raped.' It was the first time she had acknowledged the deed out loud.

'Dear God.' Laura's face whitened. 'Poor Lucy. Have they caught the man?'

'No. And she can't tell them much.' And then it all poured out. It was such a relief to tell someone who was not a police officer. 'She was supposed to be meeting Sam Jago and that's who I thought she was with. When she didn't come home by ten-fifteen – ten was the time her father had arranged to phone her and she always made sure she was there for his calls – I rang Joyce. Neither she nor Sam had seen Lucy all day.

'I didn't know what to do. I mean, the police wouldn't have done anything, not right away because she's seventeen, but I was worried sick.' Gwen explained how Lucy had arrived home. 'I rang the police immediately. It was awful, she had to have tests and things. You'd think she'd been humiliated enough.'

'It has to be done,' Laura said gently.

'I know.' And for the first time Gwen Chandler began to cry.

'Please don't tell anyone,' she said when she was calmer. 'It was in the paper on Tuesday and the *Cornishman*'ll carry a report on Thursday, but they're not allowed to print her name.'

'Of course I won't say anything,' Laura reassured her, feeling much as Gwen did, that there was little she could offer in the way of comfort.

When Gwen had gone, Laura wanted nothing more than to ring Rose. She would not break her word but she, too, needed a friendly ear. But Rose was going to a funeral that afternoon, it would be unfair to burden her with another problem even if she couldn't say what it was.

The subjects both for the class and her pupils' homework had been planned. Feeling pleased with some of the photographs she had taken on Monday, Rose decided she had time to show them to Barry and find out which of them he wanted.

The old-fashioned bell tinkled as she pushed open the shop door. There was no sign of Barry, and a woman she had never seen before stood behind the counter serving two German tourists with maps of the area.

'Can I help you?' she enquired with a smile as she handed the tourists their change and their goods in a striped paper bag. They now stood to one side looking at postcards.

'I was hoping to see Barry actually.'

'Ah, he's over at Camborne. Is it important?'

'Not really. Will you tell him Rose called in and ask him to give me a ring? And would you mind giving him these photographs, please?' She handed over a padded envelope.

'Of course. Does he have your number?'

'Yes.'

The woman frowned. 'You're not Rose Trevelyan, are you?'

'I am.'

'You're the one who does all the notelets and things. He's told me about you.'

Has he indeed, Rose thought. But he hasn't mentioned you. Which was odd, since Barry normally discussed his every move with Rose.

'You paint as well, I believe.'

'Yes.'

Another customer had entered the shop. 'Nice to have met you. I'll pass on the message.'

'Thanks.' Rose said goodbye and squeezed past the Germans who were blocking the doorway.

Barry telephoned not long after she arrived home. 'I'm still at Camborne,' he said, 'but I got your message.'

'Indeed. So who's the lady?'

'Didn't I tell you?'

'No, you didn't, or I wouldn't be asking.' She vaguely recalled him mentioning he had taken out an advert in the local paper but hadn't imagined he would actually take someone on.

'Her name's Daphne Hill. I've taken her on on a full time basis.'

'Good for you. It's about time. Tell me about her.' Maybe now Barry would find the time for a hobby.

'She lives somewhere out near Madron, but she's got a car. Her children have left home and she was bored and wanted a job.'

Rose could understand that. And Barry had been sensible in his choice. Older women tended to be more reliable, more grateful for employment, and with a grown up family there was not the problem of school holidays or sick children to care for. Rose, with her artist's eye, could have described her exactly; full-figured, handsome-featured, smartly dressed, short fair hair, make up a little on the heavy side and plenty of costume jewellery. A woman who believed in making an effort to dress well for work. 'So what'll you do with your new found freedom?'

'I haven't decided yet, well, apart from some decorating, and, if you're up for it, I could do with some help in choosing new furniture.'

'I'd love to help. There's nothing nicer than spending other people's money. It'll have to be next week, though.'

'Next week? Good God woman, I haven't even picked the paint yet. Next month, more like it.'

'That's fine. Look, Barry, I'll have to go, it's Phyllis's funeral this afternoon.'

'Sorry, I forgot. I'll speak to you soon and let you know about the photographs.'

Rose glanced at the small carriage clock on the mantlepiece. It was time to change before she went to collect Doreen.

The weather was far from funereal. The sun shone and birds sang in the trees surrounding the graveyard. Their dark coloured clothing was uncomfortably warm as Rose and Doreen walked along the path to the small church. Organ music could be heard from inside. The church was almost full. Phyllis Brown had lived in the area all her life and had known many people although none had been close friends. Only Doreen had taken pity on the woman who was renowned for her sharp tongue, her amazing organisational skills, her obsessive church attendances before her illness, and her pride. Nathan was illegitimate but Phyllis had given birth to him then held up her head and got on with life, uncaring of what people thought forty years ago – when illegitimacy had been considered shocking and a stigma to both mother and child. As if to make up for her one aberration she had turned to religion and strived for a life of cold, clean purity. She had expected the same of her son who had remained at home with her. When she became ill he did everything for her except the things which required the services of the district nurse. He had given up his job on a farm in order to do so. Rose noticed him at the front of the church, hands clasped between his knees, his head bent. It was unclear whether he was praying or crying.

The coughing and rustling stopped as the coffin-bearers entered and walked slowly down the aisle. They placed the remains of Phyllis Brown on the trestle in front of the altar and left unobtrusively.

Rose joined in the service enjoying listening to the Cornish voices rising and falling as they sang the hymns. She was aware that Nathan's lips didn't move, that he seemed to see or hear nothing.

They followed the coffin to the graveside and the clergyman spoke the ritualistic words. Automatically, Nathan picked up a handful of dirt and threw it onto the sturdy coffin which had been lowered into the ground. There was no sign of emotion on his almost unlined face.

He must take after his father, Rose thought, watching him. Phyllis had been tall and thin, her son was short and stocky with the swarthy colouring of a Cornishman whose family went back many generations.

People began to file away. Nathan had left the arrangements to his aunt, Emily, who had not thought to organise food and drink back at the house. In her eighties, coping with the other arrangements and seeing to Nathan had been more than enough for her. Belatedly, she had rung the landlord of the pub nearest to the church and asked if he could provide some sandwiches. 'I'm going back to Truro tomorrow,' she told Doreen who had gone over to speak to her and introduce her to Rose. 'Can you keep an eye on him?'

Nathan stood staring down into the open grave, aware that the grave-diggers were waiting to fill it in. In the peaceful, pretty surroundings it seemed incongruous that a bright yellow bulldozer stood waiting to do the job.

'Course I will, maid, don't 'e worry about that. Will he stay on at the house?'

'Yes. Phyllis owned it. From what I can gather from her papers she's left everything to him. He'll be all right.'

Rose, watching him, thought it would be a while before he was. Nathan's whole body shook and he had not spoken a word to anyone. How must he feel to be on his own after forty years? she wondered. Doreen had told her there were no girlfriends, no friends at all. 'She won't let 'im take no one home. Rules 'im with a rod of iron, she does,' she had once said. 'He goes along to church of a Sunday but he don't believe, he only does it to keep her quiet. It's no life for a man, Rose, take my word for it.'

Would he, now that he had some freedom, make up for the past? Doreen would certainly keep her informed. 'Nice to have met you, Mrs Davey,' Rose said. Phyllis's sister wasn't showing any signs of grief but the elderly often didn't, they just took death in their stride knowing that it would soon be their turn.

'Come back and have some tea if you're not going to the pub,' Doreen said. 'My Cyril will be gladdened to see you.'

'Just a quick cup. I've got my classes tonight.' Rose was surprised at the sadness she felt. Phyllis may have been a sharp-tongued woman but she had done what she thought was best for her son and, seemingly, had never strayed from the path of virtue after that one mistake which had changed her life.

There wasn't time to do much more than make a few telephone calls and change into jeans before she left the house again.

In the winter the gallery annexe was draughty but now the evening sun streamed in through the high windows and emphasised the dust motes floating in the air. Despite her sadness at Doreen and Nathan's loss, the class went smoothly and her star pupil of the moment, Joyce Jago, had brought in an excellent piece of work. It was a general class. Rose taught the basics of various forms of art using different materials, but she took Joyce aside that evening. 'Look, have you thought about concentrating on abstracts? You're good, you know. Your use of colour and application of paint is excellent. I can put you in touch with someone who can help you more than I can.'

'Thanks, Rose, but it's just for fun. I enjoy your classes.' Joyce sighed.

Rose was disappointed but she understood not everyone shared her passion. 'Is anything the matter?'

'Children. Who'd have them?'

'Sam?'

'Yes. She's so quiet lately and I can't get her to talk to me. We used to be so close. Her father says it's her age, but she's seventeen, Rose, not fourteen. Something's bothering her, I just wish she'd tell me what it is.' Joyce was not ready to admit that the police had paid them a visit. A female officer had assured her that Sam wasn't in trouble, they merely wanted some information from her. Joyce had guessed Lucy was somehow involved but Sam was not prepared to discuss it.

And before she could stop herself, Rose was saying, 'Would you like me to talk to her?'

'Would you?' The relief faded from Joyce's face. 'But she's only met you once, what excuse could you give?'

'I expect I'll think of something.' And with that on her mind Rose walked home.

The following morning Laura rang. 'Have you seen the *Cornishman*?' she asked.

'Yes. Which bit of it?'

'Bottom of page one and continued on page two.'

'The rape?' It had upset Rose that someone so young had been subjected to such an ordeal. David, and her few subsequent lovers, had always treated her with respect. 'Why?' Then she remembered that Jack had asked if she'd read Tuesday's edition of the *Western Morning News*. Was the girl someone she knew?

'What do you mean, why?'

'Laura, you didn't ring me up just to ask if I'd read that bit. I know you. There's something else, isn't there?' The girl was seventeen, the same age as Joyce Jago's daughter. Surely it wasn't Sam. Please, God, no, she thought before realising that it didn't make it any better whoever the girl had been. 'Shall I come over?'

'Can you spare the time?'

'Not really, but you sound as if you need to talk.'

'I know the girl,' Laura said almost as soon as Rose arrived. 'And her mother. I just can't believe it. Hasn't Jack said anything?'

'No.' But Rose understood why. The victim's name had to be kept confidential, which was why she wouldn't dream of asking Laura who it was.

'There's more to it, I'm sure. Gwen said . . . shit.'

Laura bowed her head. Her hair swung around her face as she held her face in her hands. 'Oh, Rose, I promised I wouldn't say anything.'

'You know nothing you tell me will go any further.'

Laura sighed. 'The girl is a friend of Samantha Jago. They were supposed to be together.'

Lucy Chandler, Rose thought, it has to be her. Joyce had mentioned her name and, now she thought about it, Laura knew Gwen Chandler. 'Sam's involved?' Then Joyce had cause for concern. Her daughter might even know who the rapist was if Lucy had confided in her. 'Joyce wants me to speak to Sam.' One event seemed to be touching the lives of many people.

'Whatever you do don't mention what I've told you.'

'Of course not. Look, I'd better go, Laura, I'm trying to get everything straight for tomorrow.'

She stayed another half hour but needed to get her things together for the exhibition.

At a quarter-to-five on Friday morning Rose was standing in her favourite place in the sitting-room window, drinking coffee as the sun rose higher. Sometimes, as the purple clouds of night turned into day, there would be overlapping layers of pink cloud which turned gold as they spread over the bay. Not so that morning. In a clear sky a half disc of red pushed slowly up from the horizon, its mirror image reflected in the water. As it rose higher, the full globe gradually becoming visible, its reflection took on the shape of a cone with golden ripples which elongated as the earth moved a few more degrees towards the sun. I must paint that, she thought, although with the changes coming so rapidly it would be difficult to capture. Rose inhaled deeply to fight off the nervousness she felt. Yes, it was wonderful to be having another exhibition but she was secretly afraid of adverse criticism; she still did not have the confidence to ride it out and trust her own instincts.

By six-thirty she was on her way and enjoying the experience of an almost empty road. Now and then she overtook a slow moving farm vehicle or an early bus but it wasn't until she reached Liskeard that commuter traffic, such as it was, began to build up.

With each mile her confidence grew. She was not the only artist exhibiting, she wasn't that renowned. Yet. And Geoff Carter, who seemed to know everyone in the art world, would be there to make introductions, and, as old as she was, she would be grateful for the presence of her parents.

She arrived at the hotel where she had booked a room, relieved that it had parking spaces, and found Evelyn and Arthur Forbes already there. Too excited to eat, Rose picked at the lunch they insisted upon buying, then they window-shopped in the city centre.

'We never expected to have a famous daughter,' Arthur said when they returned to the hotel to allow her mother a chance to rest before changing for the evening.

Rose laughed. 'Hardly that.'

'But you will be,' he said with certainty.

The evening passed so quickly Rose could hardly believed it had happened.

'You've sold one already,' Geoff Carter told her with a grin as he came over to rescue her from a viewer who was monopolising her.

'Which one?'

'The Zennor one.'

Rose nodded. Landscape with Sea, she had finally called it. No title had seemed apt until she realised that what might seem unimaginative was the best description of all. And it was the second most expensive. The exhibition was due to run for a month, maybe more would sell.

Empty wine glasses, paper plates and screwed up serviettes littered the tables. The crowd was thinning out. One or two had come for the free food and drink, others were there out of sheer curiosity but the core consisted of art lovers who were either genuinely interested in new work or who were hoping to make a purchase.

'Can I buy you dinner?' Geoff asked, the invitation obviously including her parents.

Rose was hungry now, she had ignored the buffet, being too busy talking to eat. 'Mum? Dad?'

'That's very kind of you, but we'll split the bill,' Arthur told him with a knowing smile for his daughter. Rose ignored it. She wasn't interested in Geoff in that way.

They found a surprisingly good restaurant and enjoyed a leisurely meal with decent wine. Rose felt a sense of anticlimax and wondered why she had allowed herself to feel so nervous. Tomorrow she would be home again and a new round of work awaited her.

They took a taxi back to the hotel. Rose kissed her parents goodnight and went to bed, relieved that their presence meant she had not had to fight off Geoff's advances and with the knowledge that she would sleep well that night.

Evelyn and Arthur set off immediately after a late breakfast. Evelyn was pale and looked as if she hadn't slept well. 'We'll make an early start as your mother's not feeling a hundred per cent,' Arthur said as he kissed his daughter goodbye. 'I expect we've overdone it a bit. Anyway, we'll ring to let you know we've arrived home safely. And make sure you drive carefully.'

Rose watched them leave. She hoped her mother was suffering nothing more serious than a summer cold.

There seemed no point in staying any longer herself. Geoff had said he was calling in at the gallery before he left and had presumably already gone there as they hadn't seen him at breakfast. Rose paid her bill and set off for home.

As soon as she arrived home, Rose unpacked her small bag then sat in the garden reading the novel she had not yet had time to finish. It revolved around a man who had murdered his mother and had, so far, got away with it. She understood why he had done so and, wondering why he hadn't done so sooner, mentally wished him luck. The sun was bright and reflected off the page. Rose closed her eyes. Her head was full of thoughts. There was Barry and his new assistant and his sudden desire to decorate his flat, Nathan with a new life ahead of him, Lucy Chandler who had been attacked and raped. And there was Jack. Jack who seemed to be ignoring her lately. Of course he was busy with the burglaries and now the rape but, knowing it was perverse of her, she still wanted to see him.

Late in the afternoon she decided to have a walk then reward herself with a drink before she went home to eat. Having got as far as the railway station she decided to continue some way along the new footpath which ran alongside it. The sea was immediately to her right. Tired but relaxed she retraced her footsteps and pushed open the door of the Yacht, a pub opposite the art deco outdoor bathing pool and built at the same time. At the bar she ordered and paid for a glass of wine then scanned the room to see if there was anyone there she knew amongst the customers. She almost spilt her drink when she saw – half hidden by a group of four men – Barry Rowe huddled in a corner with Daphne Hill who, Rose remembered, was married with grown-up children. Could she be the reason for the spending spree, the modern jackets and ties and the plans for redecoration? Not Barry, surely. You've a nasty, suspicious mind, my girl, she thought as she turned back to the bar. Neither of them had noticed her and she did not wish to cause embarrassment. It was a peculiar sensation, spotting him with a woman; not jealousy, she had always hoped he would meet someone, but surprise and a touch of disbelief. Do I go over and say hello? she wondered. They looked deep in conversation. She finished her drink quickly and left without either of them having seen her.

It was now twenty-five to seven. The shop would have closed an hour ago. The logical explanation was that Barry had offered to buy Daphne a drink to mark the end of her first week working for him. Except it was out of character. Half puzzled, half amused, Rose made her way home slowly.

I almost forgot, she thought, as she stood to clear the table after she had eaten. There was a fête in Hayle tomorrow afternoon, one of numerous such events which took place in the summer in aid of local charities or to help fund a new church roof or playgroup. She had promised Doreen Clarke, one of the organisers, that she would attend, although she doubted that her purchases of home-made chutney or a cake and a raffle ticket would swell the coffers required to redecorate the village hall.

I might as well see if Barry wants to come with me, she thought, trying to ignore her ulterior motive for phoning. She dialled the number and was surprised when he answered. There were no sounds to suggest he wasn't alone, nor did he mention where he'd been.

'Yes, why not?' he said. There was no mention of Daphne Hill either.

Curiouser and curiouser, she thought as she replaced the receiver. Maybe he'd tell her about it tomorrow.

CHAPTER FIVE

On Sunday morning Jack was still working on the Lucy Chandler case. 'Oh, bugger it,' he swore as the realisation hit him. Lucy Chandler's mother had assumed the girl was with her friend Samantha Jago, to whom they had now spoken and Jack had suddenly remembered that Rose knew Samantha's mother, Joyce Jago. Joyce was one of her pupils and Rose had mentioned her name several times as being one of the few with natural talent. And if Rose knows Joyce Jago there's nothing to stop her finding out the rest. Please, please let her stay out of it, he prayed.

They had a list of sex offenders but the profile didn't fit any of them. 'Lucy Chandler was in the pub with her boyfriend and they had a row,' Jack informed his team. 'She walked off and left him intending to make her way to the bus-stop on the main road, which explains her whereabouts at the time. Our problem is that she won't give us the boyfriend's name.' There was a possibility that he was the rapist and she was protecting him, because it was her mother who had called the police, or there might be another reason.

'Perhaps he's married. They had a row, she leaves the pub, he follows her in his car and rapes her,' one of the team suggested.

'It's possible.'

Time was passing. A week, in fact, had passed and they weren't getting anywhere, and they might not proceed at all unless Lucy Chandler was more forthcoming. The WPC hadn't got anywhere with her but they would have one more try. He was more than aware that she was the victim so they had to tread carefully. And if her account of events was true and she hadn't seen her attacker, she couldn't be of much help. But without her assistance they didn't stand a chance of catching anyone.

And then at nine-thirty on Sunday morning the telephone rang. 'Sir, there's been another one, about half an hour ago. Not so serious this time, the girl managed to get away but the MO fits.'

There would be no getting away by lunchtime after all, and no seeing Rose that day either. Despite his problems, Jack was missing her badly.

For once the weather was perfect for an outdoor gathering. So many fêtes were rained on. Sunshine flooded the countryside as they drove towards Hayle. Light reflected off the estuary as the water flowed out to sea exposing the mudbanks where waders fed in winter. There were none now, only large flocks of gulls huddled in the middle where the mud was raised and the water ebbed slowly around it and a couple of oystercatchers at the edge, their black and white plumage easily identifiable even though their long, orange beaks were sunk deep in the mud. In the winter their numbers would be doubled by others from Iceland and the Faeroes. 'A parcel,' Rose said, nodding towards the estuary.

'Pardon?'

'I bet you didn't know the collective noun for oystercatchers is a parcel.'

Barry stared at her as if she was mad. 'No, I didn't, actually'

They could hear the band as they approached the manor house in whose grounds the fete was being held. Many local dignitaries obliged in this way, opening their grounds to the public to allow charity events to take place. Bunting and banners adorned the trees which lined the drive. Rose followed the home-made signs directing her to a piece of grassland where she could park. Barry's car was in for repairs and would not be ready until Tuesday.

The lawns were crowded. The school band, like so many in Cornwall, sounded far more professional than anyone unused to the area might have expected. Most children were taught to play an instrument and schools had their own bands, just as every town and village had its own adult band or choir.

Stalls had been set up around the perimeter of the lawn. They held home-made goods, local arts and crafts, tombolas and bric-a-brac. Barry led Rose to the first stall. 'A pound's worth, please,' he said as he handed over his money and got Rose to pick five straws from a bucket. Inserted in each was a rolled-up ticket. She pocked them out with the stick she had been given but none ended in a nought or a five.

'Better luck next time,' the plump, jovial man said as he threw their losing tickets in a bin.

'We'd better say hello to Doreen,' Rose said.

They found her behind a trestle table upon which the raffle prizes were displayed. They watched as she bullied people into parting with their money. Doreen saw them and smiled wanly. She looked tired and sad. The fête would only distract her from the death of her friend for the afternoon. 'We'll take a pound's worth of tickets each,' Rose told her.

'Good for you, maid. I hope you win. 'Tis hard to get twenty pence out of some of they. Nice to see you, Barry. Are you well?'

'Yes, fine, thanks.'

'Mrs Pascoe's in a fine state. One of her boys fell over this morning and she was so busy cleaning him up that she forgot about her cakes and two of her sponges were zamzoodled. She's scraped the brown bits off and iced 'en but she's afraid for her reputation now. No one can make a sponge like she do. I don't suppose you'd . . .'

'Yes, of course.' Rose smiled at Barry conspiratorially. Message understood, she thought. She'd buy the two cakes sitting unobtrusively at the back of the stall, one iced in virulent pink, the other more tastefully in lemon and white. Laura would be the recipient. She ate anything and everything, especially where sugar was concerned. Admiring the buns and cakes which had not been overcooked, she became aware of someone standing behind her. 'Dave,' she said in surprise when she turned around.

'Hello, Mrs Trevelyan. We're here under Doreen's orders.'

'Aren't we all? This is my friend, Barry Rowe. Barry, this is Dave Fox.' She almost added my gardener but realised it would have sounded patronising or condescending.

Dave shook Barry's hand. 'And this is Eva.' Beside him stood a stunning woman in her twenties. Her dark brown hair was long but cut in raggedy layers. The waves framed her striking face. Her dark eyes were large and the expression in them hinted at both sadness and laughter. She was endowed with a sexual allure that even another woman couldn't possibly miss. Her tiers of clothing seemed to have been thrown on with complete disregard for fashion but somehow it worked.

'Dave told me that you're an artist,' she said. Her voice was low and deeper than Rose had expected.

'Yes, I am.' She smiled. 'Well, we'd better have a proper look around or Doreen'll never forgive us. Nice to have met you.'

They stayed for another twenty minutes then

went to say goodbye to Doreen. 'Can I tempt you with another ticket before you go?'

Rose reached for her purse. Doreen had promised to keep any prize they may win. 'Is something the matter?' she asked Barry as they made their way back to the car. 'You've been very quiet today.'

'I'm not sure.'

'Want to talk about it?'

Barry shrugged then pushed his glasses up his nose. 'It's probably nothing.'

'Shall we have a walk then?' They could drive to the Towans. There were three miles of white, powdery sand stretching all along the shoreline topped by hillocks of sand held together by marram grass. Amongst these dunes were chalets in which some people lived all year around and others used only for their holidays. Even in the height of summer the beach, because of its vast expanse, never seemed crowded. And there were no amenities nearby; no amusement arcades, no ice-cream sellers or cafes, nothing except the breathtaking beauty of unspoiled scenery. But before you reached it there was the run-down harbour area of Hayle to pass through.

'The Towans it is then.' Barry looked down at his brown laced shoes.

'You can take them off,' Rose suggested.

He looked vaguely shocked, as if she'd told him to sunbathe nude. In all the years she had known him he had never exposed more than his forearms.

She parked at the top of the hill and having no such inhibitions herself, removed her sandals and carried them by the straps. Barry followed her down the narrow, sandy track until they reached sea level. A slight breeze blew in their face and scattered minute grains of sand at their feet. The air was so clear they could see for miles. The turquoise water was edged with a frill of white spume as it ran slowly in and out over the beach. For several minutes they strolled without speaking, enjoying the warmth of the sun on their faces.

'Okay, out with it,' Rose finally said. There was no one around, only two small figures ahead in the far distance and a couple of families they had left behind. The only sounds were those of the gently lapping water and the scrunch of their footsteps in the wet sand by the tideline, the fine grains of which massaged the soles of Rose's bare feet.

'It's Daphne,' he began.

For the second time Rose wondered if he was having an affair with her.

'I took her for a drink after work last night. A sort of celebration that she's done so well in such a short time. Anyway, she chose that moment to come out with her confession.'

'Confession?' Rose was intrigued but deduced nothing from Barry's profile.

'Yes. It's her husband, you see. Before they moved down here he was a teacher but there was some scandal about him and a fifteen-year-old girl. Daphne said all charges were dropped but he knew he couldn't stay on at his job, there would always be too much speculation, and that he'd never get another one teaching.

'Well, she insisted I knew in case it came out anyway. She was afraid I'd ask her to leave, which of course never crossed my mind.'

Schoolgirl. Scandal. Surely Daphne's husband wasn't the man who had attacked and raped Lucy Chandler? It would be a long line of coincidence: Laura knew Lucy's mother, Lucy was the friend of Joyce Jago's daughter and Barry was possibly the employer of a rapist's wife. But the community was so small and so closely knit that although it seemed improbable it certainly wasn't impossible. However, rape was not the same thing as an affair with an underage girl. At least Daphne had had the courage to be honest with Barry. 'What'll you do?'

'Nothing, of course. Anyway, the upshot was that she's invited us to her house for a drink. I suggested Thursday evening.'

'Both of us?'

'Yes. In your case, reflected glory in knowing an artist is the motive I think, and in mine I imagine she wants me to see that her husband isn't a monster. Will you come?'

'Yes.' Nothing would keep Rose away now.

Dave arrived punctually on Tuesday morning but Rose was surprised to see Eva swing herself down from the passenger seat of the van. She had been intending to apply the pale wash to the wild flower sketches and wondered if Eva expected to be entertained.

'I hope you don't mind, Mrs Trevelyan,' she said with a smile. 'Only it's such a lovely day and Dave's going to drop me at the job centre later. I won't get in your way'

'Would you like a coffee before you start?' Rose turned to Dave who showed no sign of embarrassment.

'I'd love one, thank you. I'll just get my stuff out of the van.' He opened the back doors and took out the chainsaw. He carried it around to the back of the house then joined Rose and Eva in the kitchen. Since his last visit, the daily sunshine and a couple of heavy showers during the nights had already made the grass grow. New shoots stood tall and green amongst the shorter blades and the edges of the bare patches showed signs of new growth.

Rose placed their coffees on the table and sat down. 'Did you enjoy the fête?' she asked.

'Very much.' It was Eva who answered. 'So much hard work must go into things like that but I expect Doreen loves it.'

'You know her well?'

Eva shook her head. 'No, I've only met her a couple of times, but Dave does.'

Dave grinned and picked up his mug. There was a narrow bandage around his palm. 'A formidable lady, but kind hearted. There's always someone like that wherever you live.'

'Where do you come from, Dave?'

'Derbyshire. Wealthy rural farming stock. Born and bred into it then married into it. Oh, I'm divorced now. The life didn't suit me at all.'

'And I'm from Devon,' Eva volunteered.

'How did you meet?'

Dave picked up his mug, studied the tulips on

its sides then put it down again. He looked at Eva. She nodded, letting him know he was free to speak. 'Eva came down here to escape from a violent relationship and to decide what to do with her life. She was staying in a bed and breakfast place in Penzance which happened to be a few doors away from where I was working at the time. I saw her walking past once or twice and then we got talking, it went on from there.'

An ordinary natural progression, Rose thought.

'It was all rather sudden but I knew almost immediately how I felt about her. She's had a rough time, I wanted to try to make it up to her.'

Rose admired his honesty. Few men would be so open about their feelings. But if Dave Fox was used to living amongst a down-to-earth farming community, wealthy or not, someone like Eva must appear very exotic to him.

But Eva did not strike Rose as someone who would allow herself to be hard done by. The girl possessed a zest for life and bore none of the trademarks of a battered woman. But that was only a first impression; Rose knew better than to judge her by that. She had found a decent man, one who would care for her, the relief must be enormous.

'And I desperately need work,' Eva added. 'I can't let Dave keep me forever.'

'What sort of work?

'Anything, really, although I can't imagine spending all day in a shop or an office. I enjoy being outside too much for that.'

'Wait until you've spent a winter here, you might feel differently then. What did you do before?' Rose sipped her cooling coffee hoping she didn't appear too nosy.

'I was a croupier in a casino. Although it meant very late nights I had the day to myself. I realise I won't find similar work here. I'm looking for bar work, or something where I can do shifts. You don't know anyone who's short of staff, do you?'

'No, I don't, Eva. Sorry. But I'll ask around.' She could see that that sort of job would suit her and she'd probably be very good with the customers. The men would certainly appreciate seeing her behind the counter.

'I'll get started. Come on, Eva, you can watch me.' It was a tactful way of letting her know that Rose probably had things to do.

'Shall I wash the mugs?'

Rose suspected the offer was made because she wanted to talk. 'No, leave them, Eva. In fact, let's have another coffee then I'll go and do some work.'

But Rose did not discover what was on Eva's mind. Once or twice Eva glanced out of the window as if to make sure Dave hadn't gone, although with the constant whine of the chainsaw it was obvious he was still there. 'Were you married, Eva?'

'No. I lived with John for four years. Usual story. It was fine at first. It took me some time to realise that he was a bully, only mentally initially. I couldn't do anything right in his eyes. Once he started hitting me I knew I had to get out. He never injured me enough to need to see a doctor but I knew it would only be a matter of time. I more or less left everything behind and came down here.'

'You're surely not afraid Dave's like that.' I've gone too far, Rose realised as a fleeting expression of panic clouded Eva's lovely face.

'Of course not.'

What's worrying her then? Rose asked herself knowing she could not ask Eva.

'Is Dave coming here again?'

'I don't know. It depends how much he gets done today. Well, I have a few things I need to do . . .'

'I'm sorry. I didn't mean to detain you. I'll go and sit outside. It's a wonderful view.'

'I know. There isn't a day when I don't appreciate it.' Rose put the mugs in the sink and went up to the attic. Mixing the pale purple watercolour for the vetch she decided Eva's problem was not her concern. It was highly unlikely she would see the girl again.

Helen Trehearne had been interviewed on Sunday and again on Monday morning. She had straight fair hair, a shapely figure, an interesting rather than pretty face and came across as older than her age. 'I was walking the dog around Ryan's Field Lagoon,' she had said. 'It was about eight when I left home. I'd let Ben off his lead and he'd gone some distance ahead. I didn't see or hear anything, I had no idea there was anyone else around. And then, just as I was under the flyover, a man grabbed me from behind. He pushed me to the ground, face down. I screamed and Ben came running back barking like mad. I struggled and bit the man's hand but Ben must've scared him because he ran off. I never saw his face.'

The lagoon was man-made. It was on the opposite side of the road from Lelant Water on the outskirts of Hayle. Both places attracted bird-watchers. Behind the lagoon was a hide. It was likely that the man had hidden in it. Maybe not hidden, Jack thought, maybe he was a genuine bird-watcher who happened to see Helen and take his chance. And he's injured. Someone would notice that, surely. 'How old would you say he was?'

'I'm not sure. He felt heavy and his hands looked like those of an older man. Thirty, or forty, maybe.'

To Helen that would seem old. I must seem ancient to her, Jack thought. 'Any idea what he was wearing?'

'Yes. Jeans and a short-sleeved beige shirt. I didn't notice his shoes and I only saw him from the back when he ran away, but his hair was dark and cut short.'

A description that could fit half the male population of Cornwall. 'What happened next?'

Helen shrugged. 'I should've let Ben run after him but I was terrified. I couldn't stop shaking. I put Ben back on the lead and went home. Mum phoned you right away'

Jack asked a few more questions but the one he wanted to ask, *do you know Lucy Chandler?*, had to remain unspoken for the moment. Her name could not be revealed and the two incidents might not be connected. One had taken place outside Penzance, the other in Hayle, and Helen had received no injuries. But the dog had probably prevented that. Both she and the family refused counselling which, in Jack's opinion was sensible as it could often make matters worse. Helen promised to get in touch if she remembered anything new. Detective Inspector Jack Pearce prayed there would be no more similar incidents.

By Tuesday they were no further forward. Jack's head began to ache. A break might allow him to think more clearly. I'll go and see Rose, he thought, deciding not to telephone first in case she found an excuse to put him off. Turning up unannounced, he would at least have the pleasure of her company for a few minutes, assuming she was at home. He glanced out of the window surprised to note that the sun was still shining. He stood, grabbed his jacket from the back of his chair, checked his pocket for wallet and keys and left the building.

He started the car and headed towards Penzance. The fields on one side of the road were now in shadow as the angle between the sun and the earth was reduced but sunlight danced on the hills to his right. Clouds were gathering, not rainclouds, but large white ones which were swept along by the increasing wind until they disappeared over the horizon to be replaced by others. The long grasses in the verges swayed.

He reached Rose's house and pulled into the drive, relieved to see her car was there but aware of how often she went about on foot. But when the kitchen door opened and he saw her standing there he smiled with relief. 'May I come in?'

'Of course you can. I was just about to . . .' She stopped. Bugger it, she thought, why do I always feel the need to apologise?

Jack grinned. 'Open some wine? I was hoping you might say that.' He looked at his watch ostentatiously. 'A little late for you, isn't it?'

'I've been busy.'

'Don't snap. Where's the corkscrew?'

Rose pulled open a drawer and handed it to him. With one swift tug the cork came out of the bottle. She got out a second glass and poured them both drinks. It was her daily ritual when she was at home; work, a glass of wine as she cooked her evening meal, then another with it. 'I thought you were busy, too.'

'Rose?' He took a sip of the deep pink, almost red wine. 'It's lovely and dry.'

'It's Italian. I thought I'd give it a try.'

'We are busy. I needed to get away for a while.'

'I heard about the rape. Any idea who did it?'

'No. And now another girl's been attacked.'

'Oh, Jack.' Rose sat down and reached for his hand. For such a big, handsome man he looked momentarily vulnerable and despondent. 'Why don't you stay and have supper with me?'

'I'd like nothing more. Now tell me about the exhibition, I haven't had a chance to ask you about it.'

Rose did so, talking as she cooked, moving about the kitchen which was so familiar to her and bringing him up to date. 'Did you notice the garden?'

'No.'

'Go and have a look. It's so much lighter upstairs already. Dave said one more session will do it.'

'Very tidy,' Jack commented when he returned a minute or so later to find Rose adding capers to some fillets of fish already lying in a baking tin. She squeezed on lemon juice, added salt and pepper and placed the dish in the oven.

'Jack?' She turned to face him.

Arms folded, he stood in the doorway observing her. She was so petite she appeared delicate, although Jack knew better. She leant against the worktop, a checked shirt half in, half out of the waistband of her denim skirt, her bare legs already brown from the sun and her auburn hair falling out of the band which held it back from her face. 'Yes?' He knew something was coming, something he was sure he didn't want to hear.

'It's about these attacks. I swear I won't say anything to anyone else, but I know the name of the first girl.'

Oh, God, he thought. Not again. Please don't let Rose become involved. But he guessed it was already too late to prevent it.

'She's the best friend of the daughter of one of my students.' She did not mention Laura had given away Lucy's name.

The Jago girl had been questioned. She was supposed to have been meeting Lucy Chandler but Lucy had rung to cancel and asked her not to say anything as she was meeting her boyfriend. This seemed to confirm that the man was married. Jack knew that Rose taught Joyce Jago because she had mentioned how good she was.

'Joyce is worried about Sam, she asked if I'd have a word with her.' That was almost a week ago, Rose had been so busy she'd forgotten until now.

'She would ask you.'

'What's that supposed to mean?'

'Nothing, Rose. I'm sorry.' Everyone seemed happy to confide in Rose or to ask her to help sort out their problems.

'Does the name Helen Trehearne mean anything to you?'

Rose chewed her lip. She was aware that Jack had given her the name of the second girl. It was intentional and she knew he trusted her not to repeat it. She shook her head. 'Was she badly hurt?'

'No. She had a dog with her and managed to get away.'

'And neither of them can identify him?'

'No, but they both claim it wasn't anyone they knew. I know,' Jack held up his hands. 'How can they know that if they can't identify him? But it's clear what they mean. And we don't even know if it is one person. Let's drop it, Rose, I've had enough for one day. It's ages since I've seen you, tell me what else you've been up to?'

'The usual. Photography, sketching, the odd spot of housework, then this morning Dave came. He brought Eva with him and that put me behind even further.'

'Eva?'

'His girlfriend. She comes from Devon. Dave moved down from Derbyshire after his marriage broke up. It's odd, he obviously cares for her a great deal and I share Doreen's opinion, he's a decent man, but I got the feeling Eva doesn't trust him.'

'For heaven's sake, Rose, don't get involved in something that doesn't concern you.'

'Hardly involved, Jack. He'll only be coming back once more and then I'll probably never see either of them again. I just hope they'll be happy. At least he doesn't nag her.'

'Meaning what?'

'Meaning the way you nag me.'

'The last thing I need is a row.'

'I was making a justifiable comment not trying to start an argument.'

'Look, it might be better if I left.'

Rose reached for the wine bottle. Jack was tired and frustrated, she ought to have trodden more carefully. 'Don't go. I want you to stay,' she said quietly. 'Besides, I can't eat all that fish myself.'

Jack put his head in his hands. She had said something nice, something he wanted to hear and then she had to go and make a joke.

Over the meal the tension eased and they

talked of other things; local gossip, local news and mutual friends, including Laura with whom Jack had gone to school, but not Laura's friendship with Gwen Chandler.

When Rose mentioned that Barry had taken on Daphne Hill full-time, Jack had relaxed enough to laugh. 'I shouldn't laugh but what on earth's he going to do with himself?'

'Decorate the flat for a start, then I'm helping him choose some furniture.'

Jack raised his eyebrows. 'Changes, indeed. I had a drink with him the other evening. He's certainly smartened himself up a bit lately. All for the lovely Daphne, do you suppose?'

'No. It's nothing like that.' Soon she would be meeting Daphne's husband. She would not mention his past to Jack, it was unfair to the man and there was always the possibility that the local police already knew about it. In which case, she thought, they might also be making enquiries as to his whereabouts at the times when the two incidents occurred.

'It's a shame he can't find someone. He's a decent man, Rose, and there aren't that many around.'

She frowned, puzzled, until she realised Jack was referring to Barry, not Rod Hill. 'I know. I wish he'd find something to do that he enjoyed, other than work. But at least he's made a start.'

Rose washed up whilst Jack made coffee. The wind that had rattled the kitchen door had dropped. It was not yet dark, the summer solstice was only days away and because they were so far west light remained in the sky until almost eleven.

They took their coffee through to the sitting-room and watched the lights come on in the villages scattered along the coastline. The dusk deepened and turned the sea an inky purple. 'Bad weather to come?' Jack nodded in the direction of two large tankers and a light-ship moored in the bay. Beyond them was the silver bulk of a naval vessel, too small for a frigate but too far away to make out what it was.

'I don't know. It's pretty calm at the moment.' But seamen knew. During winter storms and summer ones there could be half a dozen or more large ships anchored in the bay, tossing, and turning but sheltered from the raging seas beyond it. 'Fancy a brandy?' She got up to pour it, thinking of Dave and Eva again. To run off like that, Eva must have been through a lot. And so has Daphne Hill, she reminded herself. Yes, it would be interesting to meet the husband. 'You won't be able to drive home now,' she said, handing Jack a cut-glass brandy balloon.

Jack grinned, deliberately boyish. 'I know, but I was hoping I wouldn't be going home, that I might be allowed to stay.'

Rose grinned back. He took that as a sign of assent.

CHAPTER SIX

Eva had been to the job centre and explained her circumstances but they had nothing to offer her. Work in the catering industry was hard to come by in the winter but in the summer, when it was plentiful, vacancies were filled as soon as they were advertised because young men and women were willing to travel from all parts of the country just to be in Cornwall for the season. 'I'll come back next week,' Eva told them, realising she might be better off looking through the adverts in the local papers.

On Wednesday she caught the bus into Penzance and started asking in various pubs if they needed any help. It was raining hard. With the drop in temperature it was difficult to believe it was summer. The hem of Eva's skirt was damp as it swung around her legs as she made her way through Morrab Gardens, disappointed that she had had no luck. She could not rely on Dave's generosity for much longer.

Despite the rain, she lingered by the fountain watching a grey wagtail who, in return, watched her. It's too good to be true, she thought, things like this just don't happen to me. Her life had been hard and she had followed the route of many. From a violent family she had moved in with a violent man but she had finally had the sense to leave him. And Dave, was he too good to be true? Where had he been on Sunday night when that girl was raped? Why wouldn't he tell her when she had asked him? There had been a closeness between them right from the start, his secrecy was out of character. He's passionate, I know that, but I can't imagine him hurting me. But maybe that was different, maybe he got his kicks in some other way. She hated herself for her doubts because she realised they were probably unfounded. If only I knew where he was I'd stop worrying. It was her background that made her suspicious, she decided. Apart from her brother the men that were closest to her had always been trouble. She did not know about the second, abortive attack.

It was peaceful in the gardens but too wet and cold to remain there any longer. She made her way down to the seafront and walked back towards the bus station. The sound of the sea, rushing shorewards on a high swell, soothed her. Dave might be at the caravan when she returned, unless he had found some indoor work. She would cook something special and try once more to find out where he had been on Sunday night.

There was no question of working outside. Rain was sweeping across the bay and running down the drive. The gutters were over-flowing, large drops of water splashed to the ground outside the window. White capped waves were beginning to form, a sign that the weather was worsening. She wondered if Dave would turn up after all. He had telephoned the previous evening to ask if it was possible to come and finish the job in the morning instead of the following week because he had been offered a week's work which he didn't want to lose. Rose had no objections; the sooner the rest of those overhanging branches were gone, the better. The van pulled into the drive. Rose heard the engine from the shed where she was stretching and preparing canvases with an old cardigan around her shoulders to keep out the chill. Although she had cleared the shed the previous year an accumulation of junk had built up again.

Dave jumped out of the driver's seat and shook his head as he glanced at the sky. Low, grey cloud was massed as far as the eye could see. There would be no let up that day.

'I'm surprised you came,' Rose said as she stood in the doorway of the shed out of the rain.

'There isn't much more to do and it's quite sheltered back there. And I've brought a petrol driven saw.'

Rose nodded. With the back of the house on one side and the granite cliff the other he wouldn't get too wet. 'Tea or coffee?'

'Neither, thanks. I want to get done quickly as possible, I've a few other things to do before I can start the job in Penzance.'

'What about your regulars?' Rose asked as he lifted his tools from the back of the can.

'I've worked it out. I can still manage to fit them in, especially now that the days are so long.'

Within minutes the noise of the saw shattered the peace of the morning. Rose went back to the shed.

Stacked against one wall were several canvases which had been blocked in. One, which had received more work than the others, showed a square built church on a bleak, gorse covered hillside and a scattering of granite cottages below it. Finishing it would be her next project.

The sound of sawing finally stopped. Dave appeared from around the back of the house wheeling a barrow full of logs. He had promised to clear away all the rubbish but Rose had said she would keep the wood to burn in the winter. He stacked the logs on top of some others already piled at the side of the shed. 'It's all done. Want to take a look?'

She did so, thanking him for what he had done. She paid him and wished him and Eva well for the future. Dave got into the van, started the engine and reversed down the drive. Rose stood watching him and waved when he reached the bottom.

Something's wrong, she thought as she went upstairs to get a warm jacket, he looks worried. But for the moment Doreen took priority. It was a week since Phyllis Brown's funeral and Rose knew that this would be the hardest time for Doreen, when the reality hit her. Apart from weekends, Wednesday afternoon was the only time Doreen was not out cleaning. Rose had rung to make sure she'd be in.

'Come on over as soon as you can, maid,' Doreen had said. 'I'm in need of a bit of company.'

It was just after two when Rose arrived. Since the day they had married, Doreen and Cyril had lived routine lives, or as routinely as possible when Cyril worked shifts in the mine. Since his retirement the pattern of their lives had become more rigid. 'It's the only way I can keep on top of things,' Doreen had told Rose although Rose suspected that the strict timetable somehow compensated them both for Cyril's redundancy and the loss of pride he had suffered when no other work was available. On Wednesdays they sat down to a cooked meal at twelve thirty, a meal which Cyril had prepared in her absence. It had taken him a long time to accept that now he was not the bread-winner he ought to help around the house. He had finally learnt to serve up meat and vegetables as expertly cooked as those which his wife had always prepared.

Rose parked in the road and pushed open the gate at the front of the bungalow. The small front garden contained a blaze of flowers which had benefitted from the rain and exuded a mixture of scents. She walked around to the back door and tapped on the glass. Behind her Cyril's vegetables stood in military rows. The runner beans, attached to poles, had a mass of red flowers and some of the beans were already forming.

'Come in out of that rain, Rose. You can't tell from one minute to the other what it'll do next.'

Rose took off her jacket and shook it. Doreen hung it on a hook on the door. The kitchen was warm and smelt of pork but there was no sign of any dishes. The fittings were old-fashioned but every surface was clear and still damp from Doreen's dishcloth. Seated at the kitchen table, Cyril was half-hidden behind a newspaper. Opposite him sat Nathan Brown.

'We made 'en a bit of dinner,' Doreen explained.

'Nice to see you, Rose, you're looking as good as ever.' Cyril put down the paper, pleased by her company. He had never known what to say to Nathan. 'I expect Doreen's about to put the kettle on?' He smiled at his wife.

'You know perfectly well I always do that, Cyril, there's no need to be showing me up. Sit down, Rose.'

It always surprised Rose when she saw Cyril without his cap. He looked years younger when his still thick hair was on display. 'How are things with you, Nathan?'

'I dunno. I can't get used to 'er not being there.'

'It takes time. It's only a week.'

'You listen to Rose. She do know, she lost her man,' Doreen said as she got out tea cups.

'I heard you're staying on at the house. Won't you find it a bit big?' It was, like many older houses in the area, built of granite. It stood in a terrace and was reached by a short flight of steps from the pavement and a path with steeply sloping lawns on either side of it. There were three bedrooms, a large front room and a dining-room. In Nathan's situation she would have found somewhere smaller and cosier and easily manageable. But when David died I knew I could never leave my house, Rose recalled. Perhaps Nathan felt the same way.

'I'll manage. Doreen says I ought to get someone in to do for me but I don't know as I can afford it yet. The lawyer's going to have a word with me next week.'

'Don't take on, Nathan. The house is paid for, it's yours now and there's a bit of money put by. You won't starve, take it from me. Besides, you're free to find work now. Why don't you see if they need you back at the farm?'

Rose was aware that Nathan had received a

small benefit payment as a full time carer. That would have stopped with Phyllis's death. She had no idea of his financial situation although Doreen seemed to. She hid a smile. There was little information to which Doreen wasn't privy, no matter how private it was supposed to be.

'Take my advice, Nathan, start looking right away. It'll give you something to do and take your mind off your mum.

'He's not been hisself at all,' she added turning to Rose as if the forty-year-old man was no more than a child.

And nor have you, Rose thought, catching the fleeting expression of pain which crossed Doreen's face. She couldn't make Nathan out. Despite his recent bereavement there was an expression of quiet determination on his face. Doreen seemed to be worrying unnecessarily. But it was early days, a time of numbness; there would be worse to come. She did not suggest that he saw a doctor as she had done after David died. After ten days and at Laura's insistence, Rose had succumbed and seen her GP. She had tried to drown her sorrow in wine but it had only exacerbated it. Nathan, loner that he was, would come to terms with his loss in his own way.

Rose accepted the tea Doreen handed her. It

was dark and strong and had been made with loose leaves. Nathan sipped his tea with his right hand, his left was resting on his knees. Had there been a woman, Rose thought, or even some friends, it might have been different but Nathan Brown had spent all of his forty years devoted to his mother, a hard task-master from what Doreen had told her. What a gap it must have left in his life. I'm here to comfort Doreen, not Nathan, she reminded herself. But he had worn well and looked several years younger than the forty he had already lived. 'The fête went off well, how much money did it make?'

'Just *over* a thousand pounds. There'll be a report in the *Cornishman* tomorrow.' Doreen's pride was obvious. She deserved to feel proud, she had put much work into it.

'That's an awful lot of money.'

'I know, but we were selling raffle tickets beforehand and we had some very generous prizes donated, including a day trip to the Scillies for two on the boat. Terrible about that poor girl, wasn't it? Has Jack said anything to you?'

'No, not really.'

'I know, you can't talk about it. I just hope they catch 'en. Rape. I ask you, no one's safe any more. And I'll tell you what, I've heard a rumour that someone from round here was attacked, another girl. Helen Trehearne I believe her name is.'

'Doreen.' Cyril glared at his wife. It might not be true and he did not like to hear such gossip.

So Doreen also knew. That was the name Jack had mentioned. 'What makes you say that?'

'I know the Trehearnes. Good family. And Helen's a good girl, not like some of them nowadays. The police were outside her house the other day and she hasn't been at school this week. That Helen's a strong maid, she won't hide her head in shame and keep it a secret. I know I'm not far out, not if what her mother told Mrs Freeman is true.'

Cyril shook his head. There was no stopping Doreen. 'Shall we have some more tea? Nathan, another cup for you?'

'No. I'd best be off.' He stood, his hands in his jacket pocket. He seemed to be trembling. 'Nice bit of dinner, thanks' he said as Doreen let him out of the back door.

'I can't imagine what'll become of that one,' Doreen commented when he had gone. 'He don't make no effort, that's his trouble. Always relied on Phyllis, you see. That's why he needs a job, without her to tell 'im what to do he'll be lost.

'Cyril, I do believe it's stopped raining.'

Cyril peered out of the window. 'I think you're right. I might as well tidy the beans.'

To Rose the garden looked immaculate but the Clarkes had their own way of doing things. Doreen wanted him out of the way and Cyril was more than pleased to be so.

'Now, tell us what you know,' Doreen said as she leant on the table, her chin in her hands.

But Rose could not break her promise to Jack. As much as she liked Doreen and valued her as a friend she knew that anything she said would be repeated. Instead she turned the conversation to Phyllis and learnt a little more about the woman's personality.

No wonder Nathan's like he is, she thought as she drove home beneath the grey sky. The rain had stopped but the roads were still wet. It was a respite, no more than that, it would rain again later.

Before she reached Newlyn she had thought of a way in which she might be able to speak to Samantha Jago without arousing her suspicions. Rose rang her at five and was rewarded by an affirmative reply to her request.

It was dry when she left the house although she could smell the damp soil, and droplets of water still glistened on the grass. The earlier rain had cleared the air, it was fresh and heady as she made her way along the Promenade before turning off for the gallery where Samantha Jago was waiting outside. 'My goodness, you're keen.' Rose had not been certain she would turn up.

'Am I dressed all right?' Sam was wearing a long, black skirt, clumpy shoes and a top which left an inch of midriff exposed.

'Of course. It's only your face they'll be interested in.' Over the telephone Rose had asked Sam if she would be prepared to model for the class, head and shoulders only, in return for a small fee. The girl had great bone structure.

'I feel embarrassed already.'

'Well, don't. You'll be fine.' Rose unlocked the door. 'Come on, we've got time for a cup of tea before the others arrive.' She plugged in the kettle and dropped teabags into two chipped mugs. 'Your mum seems a bit worried about you, Sam. Is everything all right?'

Sam reddened. 'Not really. I think one of my friend's is in trouble. The police came to see me but I'm not sure why and Lucy won't return my calls. We've been friends since infants' school and it hurts that she's dropped me for Jason Evans.'

'Surely things aren't that bad?' Rose was referring to the friendship, Sam obviously didn't know what had happened to Lucy.

'They are to me. Nobody understands.'

Rose sighed. How much the young took for granted. They assumed they were the only ones who could love or be hurt or even have a sex life. 'What else is bothering you, Sam?'

'Will you promise you won't say anything?'

'You have my word.'

'I think Lucy's been raped. No one's said as much but I read that report in the paper. I was supposed to be with Lucy at the time. Anyway, after the police came and she wouldn't speak to me it just seemed to add up. I wish I could help her in some way.' She bowed her head. 'I think she lied to me. She said she was meeting Jason and that she was using me as an excuse because her mother doesn't like him. It just seems so feeble now.'

It struck Rose as odd, too. Surely no seventeen-year-old who earned her own living needed a friend to cover for her.

'What time do we start?' Sam had heard voices in the hall.

'Almost immediately. Come with me and I'll explain what I want you to do.'

Rose led her into the large studio and began arranging the stacked seats into a semi-circle. In front of them she placed easels then decided where best to seat the girl.

Sam turned out to be a good model. Perhaps her preoccupation enabled her to sit for the first hour with hardly, a movement, her profile to the class as they quietly drew it. Rose, from a different perspective, sketched her three-quarter face. 'Okay, I think that's long enough. We'll take a break now.' They always stopped for coffee half way through the class.

The silent concentration was broken. Chairs scraped and conversations broke out as people began comparing their work.

'Thank you, Sam. We all appreciate your sitting for us. Do you want to stay until the end or would you rather leave?'

'I'll go if you don't need me any more.'

Rose took her to one side and pushed a ten pound note into her hand. It had been worth it. Rose had enjoyed sketching her and she had found out as much as she wanted to know.

‘Right, let me see what you’ve done this evening then I’ll look at what you’ve managed at home this week.’

No one had quite captured the essence of Sam although Joyce had managed to portray the wistfulness in her face. It had been a worthwhile exercise, one conducted with only herself and Joyce knowing the reason behind it.

When the class finished, she put Joyce’s mind at rest by telling her that Sam was upset because Lucy seemed to favour her boyfriend’s company over her own. She made no mention of the rape.

Satisfied, Dave Fox pushed his plate away. Eva had cooked a delicious meal. She had told him how unsuccessful she had been in finding work and he’d tried to reassure her that something would eventually turn up. ‘Don’t worry about the money, Eva. Living as we do we don’t spend much. Better you get a job you enjoy rather than taking one for the sake of it.’ He smiled and reached for her hand. ‘Don’t look so glum. You’re a winner, you know, you’ll get there in the end. Look what you’ve survived already.’

Eva felt near to tears. Never had she thought she could be so happy with a man but there was a shadow hanging over it all. 'Dave, please tell me where you were on that Sunday night.'

'Why is it so important to you?'

She pulled her hand away. Surely he must have some idea why she kept asking him. 'I just need to know, that's all. I thought we'd agreed never to have any secrets. I've told you all there is to know about me, about my family and John.'

'Likewise.'

Eva nodded. Dave had explained that his marriage had gone wrong because his wife was more of a socialite than he was. 'Unlike me, Sarah was into dinner parties and attending all the local functions where the same crowd of people gathered,' he had admitted. 'She was always wanting me to better myself, whatever that might mean. Nothing I did pleased her. I'd had it. I suddenly realised that freedom was more important than appearances. I bought the van and came down here and gave her a divorce. And do you know it's the first time since childhood I've really felt happy. Strange when money once meant something to me. And now I've got you.'

But Eva had never met any of his family. She only had Dave's word that his reasons for leaving were as he had told her. Maybe there was something far more sinister behind his move to Cornwall. Damn him, she thought, damn him for making me feel like this. One simple question. If she had the answer she knew she would be either truly happy or completely devastated.

The persistent double ringing finally penetrated Jack's consciousness. Wondering if he had overslept and someone was phoning from work to find out where he was he reached out and picked up the receiver. There was no sunlight to give him an approximation of the time, only the steady hiss of rain as it fell onto the paving stones of the small patio area outside his bedroom window. 'Hello?' He half sat up. His alarm clock told him it was ten minutes to seven. In another ten minutes it would have woken him. He depressed the button to prevent it going off and listened to the news he hoped he would never hear. If gloomy daylight had not penetrated the bedroom curtains he would have believed it to be a nightmare. 'I'll be there as soon as possible.' He replaced the receiver.

With no time for coffee, Jack showered and shaved quickly, threw on the clothes he had worn the previous day and went out to the car. Rain pounded metallically on its roof and rivulets of water ran down the road, nestling into the kerbs before disappearing into drains. Ahead the sea was a turbulent green. Don't let it be true, he thought as he started the engine, knowing that it had to be.

Belinda Greenwood was short and plump with grey hair cut like a man's. She was in her seventies and lived alone. Jack studied her. Had she been born some decades later she might well have lived openly with another female. As it was, her dog, Truffle, was her only companion. Winter or summer, no matter what the weather, she walked him several miles in the morning and another mile at night. Jack's eyes dropped to the large animal sitting obediently at her feet. It looked too old for such exercise, but so did its mistress.

Jack had driven straight to the scene of the crime and witnessed, second-hand, what Belinda Greenwood had come across when she was walking her dog at six-thirty that morning. The body of Nichola Rolland lay sprawled amongst the sand dunes, patches of fine sand adhered to her saturated clothes. She was fully dressed from the waist upwards; T-shirt, short, tight fitting mock leopard-skin jacket, earrings and a necklace. Below the waist she was naked. Her canvas shoes, skirt and knickers were scattered to one side of her. The attack had been frenzied, she'd hardly had time to struggle. The marks around her neck showed she had been strangled and the Home Office pathologist's initial examination showed she had been raped, or had had sexual intercourse not long before she died. But Nichola Rolland lay on her back, she would have been able to see her attacker which may have been the reason he had killed her. Unless his needs were escalating. The thought made Jack feel sick.

Belinda Greenwood seemed almost unmoved by what she had come across on her morning walk, but the older generation never ceased to amaze Jack. Perhaps having lived through a world war and surviving hardships the younger generation couldn't begin to imagine had something to do with it, but people of her age rarely showed the ridiculous excesses of emotion displayed by young men and women who had never suffered at all.

'I always leave the house at six-fifteen,' Belinda said. 'Truffle doesn't like his routine to be upset. We don't always go the same way, I like to vary my route.' They had walked along the shoreline then turned inland and up through the dunes. There, hidden amongst the sand and clumps of marram grass, she had spotted the girl's naked limbs. 'It was obvious she was dead. I felt her pulse, just in case, but other than that I didn't touch her or move anything. I went straight back home and telephoned you.'

Jack nodded his thanks. The woman had done the right thing. He had been contacted as soon as her call had come in. Belinda Greenwood had taken the officers who called at her house straight back to where she had found the body. Nichola Rolland had not been robbed. Her handbag was close by, there was money in her purse. The pathologist had been vague as to the time of death because no one knew when it had started raining again and the weather made all the difference. The more detailed examination which was to come would tell them more. But what, Jack thought, had she been doing out so early? Or had she been killed the night before? If it was the latter, why had no one reported her missing? He answered the question himself. Nichola's driving licence showed she was eighteen. She might live alone, or if she still lived at home her parents probably realised the police would do nothing because she was no longer a minor. But surely someone would have worried; after all, there had been two other cases. Not for one minute did Jack believe that Belinda Greenwood had murdered the girl but she still had to be questioned. They certainly needed a quick solution now. And they needed to know if the three crimes had been committed by the same person.

Back at the station Belinda Greenwood answered the relentless questions calmly and intelligently. At half-past two an officer drove her home.

CHAPTER SEVEN

The attack on Helen Trehearne had been reported in the local paper but the murder of Nichola Rolland was not yet public knowledge, not as far as the media was concerned. For the population of Hayle it was a different matter. Miss Belinda Greenwood had given her word she would not talk to anyone about what she had seen, and she kept it. But who, in an area where the presence of a police car was a rare occurrence, could fail to notice the presence of several – all heading in the same direction? It did not take long for word to spread that something serious had happened. 'The Towans, that's where they're heading.' This information was passed from person to person, the early risers who were out and about by seven o'clock. By the time the shops opened there were few who had not heard the news. The general consensus was that someone was dead.

Immediately after breakfast, Doreen rang Rose to pass on the information. 'Cyril popped down for 'is paper, just like he always does and he heard it in the shop. Of course, we don't know for certain but he was told there were about ten cars heading out that way.'

Rose knew that the latter comment was an exaggeration, maybe the former was, too, maybe a chalet had been broken into. Jack had said they still hadn't caught whoever it was burgling properties in the area.

'You don't sound shocked, maid.'

'Well, Doreen, as you said, nothing's certain yet. No doubt we'll hear about it later on the radio.' She sincerely hoped that her friend was wrong.

Disappointed at the reception of her news, Doreen hung up. She would discuss it with Mrs Patterson whose house she was due to clean that morning.

Daphne Hill said goodbye to Barry, took the car keys from her bag and unlocked the sensible saloon which was parked in the lane behind the shop.

She drove home carefully to what had once been a farmhouse. When the last but one owner had died, his son, who lived out of the county and who had no intention of ever living in it, had come down and sold off the land in parcels before having the house renovated and selling that too. The land now belonged to neighbouring farms and was still in use, therefore they had no near neighbours. For this Daphne and Rod were grateful. They had had enough of neighbours to last them both a lifetime. Had they not moved, the scandal was something they would never have been able to live down. They had chosen Cornwall as a place where it was unlikely anyone had heard of them. Even now, even though no one had been able to make the charges stick, Daphne occasionally had niggling doubts about her husband's innocence and despised herself for doing so.

The wooden gate stood open, they never bothered to close it. Daphne turned into the drive and pulled up close to the space where Rod usually parked his motorbike, an acquisition he had always wanted and purchased just after the move. It wasn't there. Just as she was putting her key in the lock of the front door she heard its engine.

'I thought I'd be home before you,' Rod said without a trace of guilt as he dismounted. He removed his helmet and bent to kiss her cheek. 'I forgot about the wine until just now.' He reached into the plastic box at the back of his bike and took out three bottles of wine carefully wrapped in tissue paper then turned and smiled. 'The job seems to be doing you good, love. You look really well again.'

'You really don't mind about it?'

'Of course not. Do you know you're a different person already?'

'It is doing me good.' It gave her a reason to dress up and put on make-up and it got her away from the house where their children had never lived, had never even visited, and where she tended to find needless housework to occupy her.

Rod hung his leather jacket in the cupboard under the stairs and Daphne went out to the large kitchen, beautifully modernised by the builders the farmer's son had employed. In her lunch hour she had bought some crisps and peanuts and a few other bits to put in dishes. They would eat properly later, after their guests had gone. Next year there would be vegetables from the garden Rod had laid out in the patch of land which came with the house. As she carried the bowls through to the lounge she wondered if Rod was behaving oddly lately or whether it was her imagination. Perhaps, despite what he said, he didn't like her working. Maybe he was missing her during the day, possibly he was jealous that she had found employment. She also wondered where he had been that afternoon, why it had taken him all day to remember to buy the wine. She could have done so herself, she had the car, but Rod had volunteered. 'I hope we've got enough shorts in the cupboard.'

'We have. I've checked, and mixers. But one of them'll be driving so I shouldn't worry about running out.'

Daphne and Rod were the same age but he had worn better. He was stocky but there was no fat on him, his hair was still thick and he had a lopsided, boyish grin which appeared between his neatly trimmed moustache and beard. Daphne took care of herself but she knew there were times when she looked older than him. Which was why she never allowed herself to take him for granted.

Rod had opened the red wine, the white was in the fridge. Money was tight, but not unbearably so. Rod had wisely invested in pension schemes and the farmhouse had cost less than the amount they had sold the house in Somerset for. And now there were her wages which she intended to save to pay for luxuries. 'Are you happy here?' Daphne asked as she folded some paper napkins.

'More than I expected to be. I thought I'd miss work and our friends.' He stopped. No, not friends, not one of them had stuck by them. In the end, without exception, they had been prepared to believe the worst or had acted on the basis that mud sticks. 'It's surprising how much you can find to do.' He laughed. 'I would never have pictured myself digging trenches and planting shrubs.'

'Me neither. And you're certain you don't mind about my job?'

'Positive.'

Rod would never go back to teaching again and, even if he tried his hand at something different, at fifty-one he would probably be considered to be too old to be employable. It was such a waste when people who had reached that age had a wealth of experience behind them.

'Shall we go for a run in the car tomorrow if it's fine?'

'Yes, I'd like that. How about Looe, we haven't been there yet?' There were still so many lovely places left to visit. The beauty of their surroundings went some way towards making up for what they had lost.

'Good idea. I believe it's jam-packed in the height of the season, now's the best time to see it.' Rod was pleased that Daphne had a weekday off to compensate for the Saturdays she would be working. It meant they could visit places when they were less busy. 'I heard a car. That must be them.' Rod turned to his wife. He knew why the invitation had been issued. Daphne had told Barry Rowe about his past and she wanted to prove that he wasn't some sort of perverted monster. He reached out and held her arm as she started to walk out of the room. 'You do believe me, don't you, rather than what that girl said was supposed to have happened?'

Daphne nodded but she did not stop walking. Rod let go of her arm.

Rose watched the wild tossing of the sea through a curtain of rain. A summer storm, no unusual thing, and they were frequently followed by warm, dry weather. It had been building up to this for days. The waves rolled in relentlessly. In another hour they would be splashing over the Promenade, the road might even be closed.

Not expecting any visitors, she didn't bother

to dress. She made coffee and watched the yucca at the side of the garden as all three trunks of the twelve foot plant bent in the wind. Beside it a small fir shook as if it had St Virus's Dance. The storm raged around the house but Rose, in her towelling robe, was warm, and she had put the heating back on a low temperature.

She took the coffee up to the attic and began to work on the watercolours. It would take most of the day but half of the job would be completed. Three more wild flowers were needed to complete the set but she hadn't got around to sketching them yet.

It was a quiet, peaceful day. The phone didn't ring and no one disturbed her. Later, she lay in the bath feeling she had achieved something. Only then did she recall what Doreen had told her that morning but she had not listened to the news all day. If it was true then Jack would be rushed off his feet. She was ready to go out but there was another hour or so before Barry was due to collect her. His car was now back on the road. Rose sat on the window seat and watched the rain clouds roll away to reveal a blue sky. The coastline in the distance gradually became visible again and seagulls, which had flown inland to avoid the storm were now wheeling over the bay. How different was the view from the morning.

She picked up the novel she had not had time to finish and read the last twenty pages. So he got away with it, I knew he would. I wonder how many people murder their own mother? Her thoughts led to Nathan, who definitely had not committed matricide, before she heard Barry's car.

'It's a bit better now,' he commented as he opened the passenger door for her.

'Yes. And you're looking rather dapper.' New shoes, dark brown trousers, a cream shirt and a brown and green checked sports jacket. The colours were coordinated and suited his sallow complexion.

'Dapper? Honestly, Rosie, you come out with the quaintest words at times. What's wrong with stylish or even handsome? No, forget the latter.' He grinned and got in beside her. 'I bought some wine. I'm not sure of the etiquette of occasions such as this.'

'It can't do any harm. It didn't cross my mind actually. Do you know how to get there?'

'Daphne gave me clear instructions.'

They had missed the after work traffic and realised with such a short journey they would be early. Barry negotiated the narrow, twisting lanes and squinted at a sign. 'That's it. She said to turn right here.'

They bumped down a rutted lane, the ruts now filled with muddy water. Barry sighed. The car had been returned to him clean; it would now be splattered with filth.

The gate was open. Ahead was a large, rectangular building which must once have been a farmhouse. Around it were fields, some used for grazing land, and in front was a newly laid out garden. Birds sang in the trees and cows lowed behind the hedge but there was no barking dog to welcome them. Rose sniffed. She had never admitted she quite liked the healthy, grassy smell of cow dung.

The front door opened before they reached it. Rose recognised Daphne immediately. Both women smiled. 'Come on in, we're glad you could make it.' She made it sound as though this was some sort of celebration. 'Rod, Barry and Rose are here. Oh,' she turned to Rose. 'I'm sorry, do you mind if I call you that?'

'Not at all.' They followed Daphne into the large lounge at the front of the house. The enormous picture windows gave a view over miles of sloping countryside. Only in the very far distance could a sliver of sea be seen.

Rod Hill stood awkwardly in front of the fireplace knowing he would be under scrutiny. Barry knew about his past but did Rose Trevelyan? He smiled and shook hands as the introductions were made. 'What would you like to drink?'

They all had wine. 'Help yourselves,' Daphne said, indicating the glass bowls of nuts and crisps and olives.

'My wife seems to have taken to shop work,' Rod said when they were all seated.

'She's ideal, a natural with the customers. And it gives me a chance to get over to the print works. This is a lovely house.'

'Thank you, but we can't take the credit for that, it was modernised before we moved in. The garden's my domain. I've made a start. It looks bare at the moment but when those shrubs start to mature it'll improve.'

Flowering shrubs, Rose noticed, although she couldn't name them as her father would have done.

'And the back's devoted to vegetables. Want to have a look?'

Rose smiled. It seemed that Rod Hill had taken to Barry. Barry put his drink on a small table and went to inspect Rod's work.

Daphne picked up an olive and chewed

it slowly wishing they'd all gone outside. 'Does . . . did . . . ?'

'Yes. Barry told me,' Rose said. 'I promise you it'll go no further. Barry's known me for years, he knew I would never say anything.'

'Thank you. I appreciate it. We both do.' She turned to look for her glass.

Rose watched her. Daphne was dressed in a similar way to the first time they had met and her hair and make-up was immaculate. But there was a jerkiness to her movements which did not seem natural to her. She picked up her glass and sipped. 'It hasn't been easy for us. Most people believed Rod was guilty. The girl lied, she was a trouble-maker and she thought it all a joke. She was too immature to realise she'd ruined two people's lives. I can't forgive her, Rose, as hard as I try. Rod will never be able to teach again.'

'The main thing is that you believe him.'

Daphne bit her lip. 'Yes,' she said. 'Yes, of course I do.' The modicum of doubt was not in her words but in her tone.

'How long have you lived here?'

'A couple of months. We're still getting used to it.'

A couple of months. And since their arrival

there had been two attacks on young girls. 'Have you met anyone yet?'

'Well, as you must've noticed, we've no near neighbours and what with getting the house ready and my finding a job, there hasn't been time. Rod goes to the pub a couple of evenings a week. It does him good. Before I started at the shop we were together all day. We both realised we needed some space.'

Rose nodded. It was natural enough but it did give him the opportunity to . . . stop it, she told herself. Don't be ridiculous. Her first impression was that Rod Hill cared very much for his wife. He did not strike her as the sort of man who would have an affair with an underage pupil, but then what man would? And he had the advantage of being mature as well as good-looking, which often appealed to young women. And the girl who had been raped had been walking not far from here. All right, the second attempt had been in Hayle but Rod possessed a powerful motorbike. But what excuse could he have given to have been absent around half-past eight on a Sunday morning? And what would Jack say now if he knew what I was thinking? Forget it, Rose, let him do the job.

There were voices in the hall. 'You should

have a go, Rose. Use one of your borders for beans or something?'

Rose raised her eyebrows. 'Honestly, Barry, I barely cope with what's in the garden now. I'd forget to water them.'

'Another drink?' Rod Hill looked far more relaxed than when they had arrived. Perhaps he had had a heart to heart with Barry or maybe the sight of his plants soothed him. 'The garden was a wilderness when we moved in. The workmen had left rubbish lying around and it hadn't been cultivated before. We got a man in to do the heavy work. Dave Fox. I don't know if you've heard of him but he came highly recommended.'

'Yes, he did some work for me, too.' Rose met Barry's eyes but he said nothing. He had no idea about her thoughts on the attacks, that she was wondering if Daphne's husband might be responsible. Now Dave Fox came into the equation. Eva gave the impression that there was something wrong and Dave Fox knew Rod Hill. One attack near here, the other in Hayle, spitting distance from St Erth where Dave and Eva lived. Now I really am being ridiculous, she thought, hoping she wasn't blushing.

Daphne showed them around the house which was roomy and decorated in keeping with the period in which it was built. It had not been spoilt. Modernisation had been restricted to the bathroom and kitchen. There were three bedrooms. Rose wondered who might conceivably sleep in the other two. Not friends from the past, they had made that much clear. Their grown-up children? Neither Rod nor Daphne had mentioned them and there were no family photographs in evidence. How sad that they had had to uproot themselves on the say so of a teenage girl. Unless, of course, she was telling the truth.

They refused the offer of another drink. Rose was hungry and Barry had to get the car home.

'What did you make of him?'

'He seemed very nice to me. It's hard to tell from one meeting though,' Rose answered non-committally.

'Poor bugger,' was all Barry had to say.

He dropped Rose at home. She had refused his offer of a curry. She needed an hour or so alone.

The light on the answering-machine was flashing. Rose depressed the button to listen to the messages. 'Hi, it's me. Gwen Chandler came to see me again today. She doesn't know what to do about Lucy. She still won't talk to anyone. Got any ideas? You're usually full of them.' It was Laura.

Rose frowned as she tried to imagine what the girl had felt during her ordeal. I hope she'll be able to get over it in time, I hope she's strong enough. Rose knew that many weren't, that the scar would last a lifetime. She would ring Laura back in the morning.

'Rose, Dad here. Can you ring me? It's about half seven Thursday evening. It doesn't matter how late it is, please ring when you get home. I'll be in from about ten.'

Rose stiffened. It was always her mother who rang then put her father on the line. But it was more than that, there had been desperation in her father's voice. She glanced at her watch. It wasn't nine yet. She picked up the phone anyway. There was no answer, apart from her mother's voice requesting her to leave a message. 'It's nearly nine, Dad. I'm at home now. I'll try again later but if you get in early please ring me.' She tried his mobile phone number but a computerised voice told it wasn't switched on. She could leave a message. Rose repeated her earlier one.

Her hunger had disappeared. She paced the sitting-room. Not even the view helped that evening. Later, she poured a glass of wine which she didn't really want but opening the bottle gave her something to do. She lit a cigarette and watched the smoke curl to the ceiling. She felt helpless. By ten-to-ten the phone still hadn't rung. She tried her parents' number once more but the answering-machine was still activated.

Finally, at quarter past ten she got through. 'Dad, what is it?'

There was a few seconds silence before he replied. 'It's your mother, Rose. She's in hospital.' It didn't sound like his voice at all.

'Oh, God. Is she all right?' Rose felt the panic rise.

'They say she's stable now. It's her heart, Rose. We had no idea. I mean, she didn't have any symptoms, she just collapsed.'

'I'll come up. If I leave now . . .'

'No, leave it until the morning. She needs rest at the moment. I stayed until they asked me to leave.'

'But what about you? Are you all right?'

'I think so. It was the shock. Anyway, June Potter's here. She offered to stay the night but I said it wasn't necessary. I'll be better off on my own tonight.'

June was a neighbour. Her parents had got on well with her ever since they had moved to the area. Rose realised there were few nights during her parents' marriage that had been spent apart.

'I'll set off first thing in the morning, Dad. I'll ring you before I get there.'

'I'll be at the hospital. Why don't you meet me there.'

Rose wrote down the name and directions. She was shaking. Naturally she knew they could not live for ever but she had never realistically faced the possibility of either of them dying. It had been different with David: his illness had lingered over several years. This time there had been no warning. She's not dead, Rose reminded herself, and treatment these days has improved tremendously – many people survive a heart attack.

She went to bed but sleep eluded her. It would be daft to set off too early, she would not be permitted to see her mother until a reasonable time. Knowing that Barry was an early riser she rang him early the next morning to tell him the news. 'Can you let Laura know? I don't want her worrying about me. Oh, and Doreen, too.'

'Of course. Give your parents my best, won't you.' He hesitated. 'What about Jack?'

'No. He's busy. I'll let him know myself when I get there.'

It had been a beautiful dawn. Orange streaks had pushed away the night sky and spread over the bay. Now the sun had risen fully and as Rose took her hastily packed overnight bag out to the car she could already feel its warmth.

The drive seemed endless. She wanted to stop and telephone her father but knew that he couldn't have his mobile on in the hospital. I just want to see her, to make sure she's all right, Rose thought.

She stopped for fuel and coffee, resenting the wasted time but knowing that a break was essential, and finally reached her destination. Having found a parking space she negotiated the labyrinth of corridors and lifts until she reached the ward. 'I'm Evelyn Forbes's daughter,' she told the sister on duty.

The sister did not smile. Rose's legs felt weak. 'You father's with her, second bed on the left.'

'Thank you.' Rose wanted to ask questions but a tearful couple were sitting in the office. They seemed to be recipients of worse news than her own.

'She's asleep,' Arthur whispered even though there was enough bustle going on around them.

Rose kissed him and sat in the chair by the bedside. She took her mother's hand. It was warm and limp. Her face was pale and she was hooked up to several monitors. At least she wasn't in intensive care, that had to mean something.

'They've told me she'll be on medication for the rest of her life.' Arthur looked near to tears. He had never seen his wife so vulnerable. 'If it works, it doesn't matter.'

They didn't talk much, just being there was enough. When Evelyn woke she smiled with pleasure to see Rose. 'You needn't have come, darling, I'll be fine soon.' But her voice was weak and she soon fell asleep again.

They stayed all day. Neither took a break to go to the canteen but the nurses provided coffee and tea from the ward kitchen. 'We ought to eat and get some sleep,' Rose suggested. 'We won't be able to help her if we're not fit.'

Rose followed her father's car to the house. Thc Cotswold stone glowed honey-coloured in the evening sunshine. Surrounding the house was the beautiful garden. The flowers were flourishing and honeysuckle filled the balmy air with its scent. The evidence of their hard work made Rose want to cry.

Arthur poured them both a drink. They sat on the rustic bench beneath the sitting-room window not knowing what to say. There was only one topic on both of their minds.

'We really must eat,' Rose said, knowing it would be difficult. She had not felt hungry since before she had heard the news.

'Yes. And then we'll take a stroll down to the pub. Everyone wants to know how she is.'

Rose cooked some pasta and used a jar of ready-made sauce to go with it. They ate in the large, sunny kitchen which had always been her mother's domain, then did the washing-up between them.

The Coach and Horses was a ten minute stroll away. People were sitting outside on the combined benches and tables. Arthur greeted a couple of them. 'She's stable,' he said in answer to their questions. Rose realised his suggestion to come to the pub had been more for his own benefit than for hers or his friends'. He had needed his daughter with him to face those questions.

By the end of the evening Rose had become reacquainted with several people she had met on previous visits, including a fellow artist. The last time she had been to see her parents he had asked her out. His invitation had been refused. 'He's divorced,' her mother had told her. But Rose hadn't been interested.

He was there again that evening but, knowing the circumstances, kept the conversation general. 'If you're here tomorrow night perhaps I could take you both to dinner,' Tony Boyd said as they were leaving.

'It's very kind of you. Maybe Rose will accept your invitation but I don't feel I'd be very good company at the moment.'

'I can't leave him on his own,' Rose said, when Arthur went out to the toilet.

'I understand. But if you change your mind I'll be here at six-thirty. I know a couple of places where we wouldn't have to book, even on a Saturday.'

Even though anxiety had exhausted them, neither Rose nor Arthur slept well that night. But they were more optimistic in the morning when they found Evelyn sitting up in bed, her glasses on, reading a book.

'You go and meet Tony,' Arthur said when they returned to the house at tea time. 'I'm quite capable of knocking up a basic meal and it'll do you good.'

'No, I couldn't . . .'

'Don't argue. Go and put your face on and have a good time. I'm going to have a quiet evening with a book.'

He looks so tired, Rose thought, and the reason she did as he suggested was because she suspected he needed some time to himself without having to make conversation.

'I'm so glad you could make it,' Tony said,

smiling widely when she appeared. 'I've got the car outside, hence this.' He touched the bottle of low alcohol beer. 'If you hadn't come by eight it would've been a different matter.'

The restaurant Tony had chosen was attached to another pub six or seven miles away. The food was average but the service was good. As they ate they talked about their respective work. It was still quite early when they began the drive back. 'Fancy a walk?' Tony asked.

It was uncomfortably warm. Rose had forgotten how humid it could be away from the sea, especially now they were into July. 'Yes, I do.'

'Then we'll stop in a minute, I know just the place.' He pulled into a lay-by. They got out of the car and followed the sign for a footpath. There was nothing to see but countryside stretching way into the distance. 'It's so very English,' Rose commented when they stopped at a style to look at the view. 'Cows and sheep, fields and trees, and all so gentle, somehow.'

'And peaceful. We seem to have the place to ourselves.' He reached for Rose's hand to help her over the steep stile. As she stepped down he pulled her to him and kissed her.

Rose gasped before responding. The kiss

lasted a long time. Tony led her off the pathway pulled her gently to the ground and very slowly made love to her. And she, amazed at herself, let him.

Afterwards, almost as if she had had an out of body experience, as if she had been watching herself from a great distance, Rose sat up and carefully rearranged her clothes. There were twigs and dried grass in her hair. Her face was flushed and there were tears in her eyes. She did not know why she was crying; whether it was because she had behaved so unpredictably, or because she had been able to feel enjoyment when her mother was lying in a hospital bed or if it was out of a sense of betrayal to Jack. If she could ever face him again she would be able to forgive him for his brief fling with Anna.

'Don't have any regrets, Rose. I've wanted to do that since the first time I met you. I don't want it to be the last time, either.' He took her hands and pulled her to her feet.

At least he doesn't look on me as a one night stand, she thought as she brushed stubborn leaves from her clothes.

'May I have your telephone number?'

She gave it to him. It would not happen again. He was nice and kind and fairly good-looking but not a man she wished to have a long-term affair with. However, he lived near her parents and there might be a time when she needed him.

And before I see Jack I have to face my father, she thought as Tony drove her home.

It had been comfort she needed, not sex, she realised, that now. But the deed had been done, she would just have to live with it.

CHAPTER EIGHT

Trevor was at sea and was not due back for another five days. Laura had half promised one of her sons she would pay a short visit. It would be good to see her grandchildren again, although they would be coming to Cornwall in August. I'm getting old, she thought. It seems such an effort to travel to Wales just for a couple of nights. It was Sunday morning, the time she made her weekly telephone call to all three sons. A decision had to be reached. But what if Rose needed her? Barry had rung with the news but there had been no word from Rose herself. Wanting to know how Evelyn was she tried to contact Rose on her father's number. No one was in so she left a message. She then spoke to her sons and their families and explained to Terry the reason for the postponement of her visit. She was trying to decide whether she felt like re-painting one of the bedrooms when the doorbell rang.

'Jack. Good heavens. Long time, no see. Come in.'

He followed her into the kitchen, ducking his head beneath the low lintel.

'Coffee?'

'If you're making it.' He pulled out a chair and sat down.

Laura noticed how tired he looked and that the lines which curved from his nose to his lips had deepened as they did when he was worried. 'It's the murder, isn't it?'

He nodded. 'Laura, has Rose said anything to you?'

'About what?'

'About any of the girls?'

Laura turned away to hide her embarrassment. It was she who had confided in Rose. Presumably Jack wasn't aware that she knew Gwen Chandler and therefore also knew the identity of the first girl to have been attacked. And she had passed this information on to Rose who had kept it to herself.

'Laura?' Jack was frowning. He saw by her face that she was trying to avoid answering him.

'All right.' She faced him, her hands on her narrow hips. 'I happened to mention to Rose that Lucy's mother came to see me. There wasn't anything wrong in that, was there? I mean, Gwen wasn't keeping it a secret and Rose always has a different perspective on things. I thought she might know how to get Lucy to talk to her mother, especially as she's friendly with Joyce Jago, Lucy's best friend's mother.'

'So that's the reason she's bloody well avoiding me. I wonder just how much Joyce Jago has confided in her. A damn sight more than in us you can bet.'

'Calm down, Jack. Rose isn't avoiding you.'

'Oh, really? Then why isn't she answering the phone or returning my calls? I've just been to the house and her car isn't there. She doesn't usually work on Sundays.'

'The reason she's not there is because her mother's ill. She's had a heart attack.'

'Oh, God.' He lowered his head. Certain that Rose had been meddling, even endangering herself, he had come to see if Laura knew where to find her. His anger evaporated. 'How is she? Evelyn?'

'I don't know.' She poured boiling water over the granules in two mugs and handed one to Jack. 'She hasn't been in touch. Barry let me know she'd gone up there early on Friday morning. He hasn't heard anything since, either, and I didn't get a reply from Arthur when I rang this morning.'

'She didn't let me know.'

He's hurt, Laura thought, and I don't blame him. I assumed Rose had asked Barry to ring him. 'I expect she was too worried to think about it.'

'Maybe.'

Laura spooned sugar into her coffee. Yes, Rose would be very worried, but was Jack right, did she know more than was good for her and was therefore avoiding contact?

'I need to know, Laura, or I wouldn't push it, has she talked to you about these girls?'

'No. Honestly. I've told you what happened, there's nothing more to it than that.'

'All right. Will you let me know if she does get in touch?'

'Of course I will.'

'Thanks. I'm taking the rest of the day off. We've got some men down from Plymouth but so far they've made no more progress than us.'

Laura knew that the body of a seventeen-year-old girl had been found amongst the sand dunes.

Because the girl had been murdered the name had been released to the press. Nichola Rolland's parents had driven down from Liskeard to identify her. How must Lucy be feeling, knowing she was lucky to still be alive? She followed Jack to the front door which opened directly onto the narrow lane.

'Got any plans for today?' he asked.

Laura shrugged. 'I was going to start some decorating. Trevor never has time for it. Somehow it seems a shame to waste this weather.'

'Why don't you join me for lunch then?'

'No need to ask twice. I'll get my bag.'

'I haven't got the car.'

'That's okay.' Laura and Trevor, like many other locals, did not possess a car. She was used to going on foot or using the regular bus services.

Laura didn't ask where they were going, she simply walked beside him knowing he needed company even if he didn't need conversation. They were heading along the seafront. There were quite a lot of people sitting beneath the shelter of the curved sea wall enjoying the sunshine. The very low tide exposed clusters of rocks and the smooth soft sand which remained below the water when the level rose. The beach was a slope of pebbles which were rearranged with the force of a rough sea; sometimes shifted into large ridges, sometimes flung over Newlyn Green. Now only a smooth blue surface could be seen as if the sea was resting.

The Promenade was busy. There were couples, young, old and middle-aged, and children on bikes or running around. Most of the people looked happy; the sun seemed to have that effect.

Laura looked out to sea. There was St Michael's Mount, its outline as familiar to her as Trevor's face. Her eyes followed the curve of the coastline. Fishing villages were tucked into the small bays and, in the distance, she could make out the satellites of Goonhilly and the sweep of land which led to the Lizard.

Jack ignored the view. He was thinking of Rose. She was so close to her parents he could not imagine what the death of one or both of them would do to her. His own father was dead but they hadn't got on. He had grieved, naturally, but not half as much as he would when his mother's life ended. She was in her seventies and lived independently but he did not know for how much longer.

They were halfway along the seafront when Jack said, 'I thought we'd eat at the pool if that's all right with you.'

'Lovely. We always do that when the boys are down.'

They stopped at a small shop to buy a bottle of wine. Laura grinned. 'I was going to suggest that myself. At least let me pay for it.'

The open-air pool was busy. It stretched out over Battery Rocks with only the sea beyond it. Children were shouting and splashing in the small pool, adults and older children swam in the irregular shaped main one. They entered the cafe gates and went up some steps to where large rope spools served as tables. Stuck in the centre holes were striped umbrellas. Everything dazzled; the water of the pool against the white walls, the spray from the splashing children and the iridescent sea.

From the hatch of a small building, chips and burgers and ice-creams were sold but also, surprisingly, Greek food: hummus and calamari, grilled sardines with appropriate salads and pitta bread. Jack and Laura opted for Greek food and asked for two glasses for their wine. The cafe was not licensed but invited people to bring their own drinks.

They sat in the blazing sun watching the activity around them as they waited for their meal.

'We've interviewed everyone connected with those three girls, it doesn't seem possible that we have no leads at all.' Jack poured the wine which the shop-keeper had uncorked for him.

'Is the same person responsible for all the attacks?'

'We have to hope so although we're not discounting more than one. What do you know of Lucy Chandler's boyfriend?'

'Not much really. He's called Jason Evans, according to Rose, and he's a year or so older than Lucy. Unemployed, according to Gwen, although he's been looking for work. Second hand information, I'm afraid. You surely don't think he raped her and that's why she's not talking?'

According to Rose, Laura had said. So Rose knew the identity of the man they had been looking for but she hadn't bothered to let him know. Rationally, he had to assume she would think they were already in possession of that knowledge. 'I don't know. Anyway, I didn't bring you here to discuss this, I just can't seem to get my mind off it. Ah, here comes our food.'

Jack's lightweight jacket hung over the back of his chair. He wore jeans and a short-sleeved shirt, pale yellow against his swarthy skin. He and Laura might have been related with their dark colouring and brown eyes. Laura was wearing a pink T-shirt and a short skirt which made her legs look even longer and thinner than they were. They ate and drank and half listened to the conversations taking place around them.

'Barry's got a full-time assistant.'

'Yes, Rose told me.'

'Daphne Hill. Barry and Rose went out to their house.'

'Did they?'

'Yes, it was all rather odd.'

'Odd?' Jack met Laura's eyes.

'Not in that way. Just sudden, I suppose. I mean, Daphne had only been working for Barry for just over a week, the next thing is they're going there for drinks. Poor Rose.'

'Pardon?'

'She hasn't had an easy couple of weeks. There was the exhibition, and you know how nervous she gets, then Phyllis Brown died and now there's Evelyn. And you know what she's like, she worries about everyone.'

'Who, for instance?'

'Phyllis's son, Nathan. And Doreen who'll miss Phyllis dreadfully. And, of course, her father. Rose's father, not Doreen's,' Laura clarified.

'Anyway, let's hope she gets in touch soon. That's the last of the wine. Shall we make a move?'

'Yes. I think I'll have a quiet afternoon in the garden.'

They walked back together until they reached the bottom of Morrab Road where Jack turned off. His ground floor flat included the back garden of the house which was mainly grass. There were flowering shrubs in the borders which required little attention, which was how he liked it. He cut the lawn at regular intervals and left it at that.

Whilst other people enjoyed the summer afternoon Jack sat and brooded about the attacks and tried to think of a reason why Rose had not told him about her mother.

Laura, having abandoned the idea of decorating, went down on the beach, leant back against the sea wall and drifted off to sleep.

On Monday morning, having been reassured the previous evening that her mother would be out of hospital in a few days, Rose drove back to Cornwall. Her father's relief at the good news was obvious and he was full of plans for the future. 'I'll do more around the house,' he told Rose as she got ready to leave. 'I'll make sure she doesn't overdo it. In fact, we could afford to have someone to come in to do the cleaning.'

Rose smiled. She knew her mother would not allow that, that once she was fully recovered she would insist upon doing her own housework, but she said nothing.

It was an uneventful journey home and much more relaxing than the one up had been.

Only when she had crossed the Tamar Bridge did she recall what had taken place on Saturday night with Tony Boyd. She felt the heat rise in her face and opened the window a little more. It seemed impossible to believe she had acted in such an impulsive manner.

The nearer home she was the more the events of the previous week filled her mind. Had Jack found Lucy Chandler's rapist? Had he arrested anyone on a burglary charge? She had forgotten the telephone call when Doreen had mentioned police cars heading towards the Towans. Jack. How can I blame him for taking Anna out after the way I've behaved? she asked herself, recalling how hurt she had been even though she had been keeping Jack at a distance. Tony Boyd had been there at a time when she needed the comfort of physical contact. It had been no more than that. She would try to put him out of her mind.

It was lunchtime when she arrived home. The sun was beating down. It was the hottest day of the year so far. She let herself in then went to collect the post from the mat and to listen to her messages. There were several from Jack. He sounded annoyed. Two concerned photographic work, which she would probably turn down, and there was one from Doreen asking her to ring. Doreen would be at work now, that would have to wait.

She was making some lemon tea before she remembered she had not returned the call Laura had made when she was away.

'Where are you? How's Evelyn?' were Laura's first anxious words.

'I'm back, and she's a lot better. They're letting her out by the end of the week.'

'Thank goodness for that. We've all been so worried.'

'We?'

'Me, Barry and Jack.'

'Jack knows?'

'Yes, we had lunch on Sunday. Oh, Rose, another girl was raped. But it's worse, this time she was murdered.'

'Oh, God, how awful.' Suddenly her head was full of things she ought to have told Jack. Did it matter if Rod Hill was questioned now? Did it matter if Dave Fox who might equally be innocent or guilty had a visit from the police if it saved another life? On the other hand, just because he had a plaster on his hand did not mean Dave had been bitten by Helen Trehearne, and she might have been mistaken about Eva's strange attitude towards Dave. But there was something amiss there, of that she was certain.

'Anyway, Gwen's coming over tomorrow and she's bringing Lucy with her. I doubt if she'll say much, but you never know.' Laura paused. 'I don't suppose you're free to come for coffee?'

Rose laughed. 'You're very transparent, Laura Penfold, but, yes, I'll come.' Now that her mother was on the mend she felt she could face anything.

'Good. About eleven.'

'What about Lucy's job? Doesn't she work in a hairdresser's?'

'Yes, but she's got a doctor's certificate. Gwen told her it was the best way to stop them from finding out what really happened.'

'I'll see you tomorrow.'

Rose made several other calls to let people know she was back and that the news was good.

'Did you hear about the murder?' Doreen

asked once she was satisfied that Evelyn Forbes was on the road to recovery.

'I did.'

'What is the world coming to? Anyway, I'm still trying to get Nathan sorted out. He refuses to have anyone coming in, he says he looked after his mother he can look after himself.'

'But surely the house is too big for him to cope with.'

'I know that, 'e just won't listen to sense. And if you ask me, that's one stubborn man. It's just sinking in, the fact that he won't ever see Phyllis again. I called in yesterday, just to take him some saffron cake, I've got some for you, by the way, and he was just sitting there, curtains drawn, on a lovely day like that. Mind you, he was clean and shaved and the house was tidy. He's moved Phyllis's bed out of the sitting-room, too. Could you have a word with him, he'd have no truck with counsellors. You've always been a one for getting people out of the doldrums.'

'I'll think about it, Doreen, I've got a few things to catch up on first.'

'Course you have, maid. I'll speak to you soon.'

Rose hung up. People did tend to confide in her, to tell her things they wouldn't tell close relatives or friends. She never had been able to understand why that should be, unless it was simply because she wasn't close. Two requests to talk to people in the short space of time since her return. What would Jack make of that? 'Damn it, I'll have to phone him,' she said, wondering why she felt so nervous. Later, she decided. He would be too busy with work to take personal calls, even if he was in his office.

She was in the kitchen making a tentative plan of where she would work which, as always, depended upon the weather, when a figure appeared in the doorway. It was Eva. *What now?* she thought irritably. I've only been back five minutes and everyone seems to need my attention. But the kitchen door was open, there was no escape. Too late she recalled Jack's advice about locking it at all times.

'I'm sorry to turn up like this, but I was in Penzance and I wondered if you'd heard about any jobs.'

Rose had forgotten she'd intended to ask around. The sort of employment Eva was after was usually gained by word of mouth. Surely she hadn't come out of her way when a telephone call would have sufficed? 'I'm sorry, Eva. I've been away. I'll let you know if I do hear of anything.

No luck at the job centre or through the paper?'

She shook her head. Even though she was troubled she was still lovely. Rose glanced at the kitchen clock. It was already after five. The afternoon had disappeared and she had had her fill of tea. 'What is it, Eva?' She looked as if she was about to start crying.

'I don't know. Everything.'

Rose pulled out a chair and sat her in it. She handed her a tissue from the box on the fridge and decided that she might as well open a bottle of Chardonnay and listen to what Eva had to say. She realised it was one of the more expensive ones she had been keeping for a special occasion. 'Tell me about it?' she said as she placed their drinks on the table and sat down. The wine was well chilled, condensation formed on the sides of the glasses almost immediately. Rose took a sip. Well worth the extra money, she thought as Eva searched for the words with which to speak.

'It's not just a job, although that's beginning to get to me. There isn't much to do at the caravan and I can't let Dave keep me for much longer.' She sighed and brushed back the dark strands of hair. 'It's Dave,' she said, very quietly. 'He worries me.'

'In what way?'

'We have no secrets. Oh, I can't expect you to believe that, but after what we've both been through, that's how we wanted it. My problem is, Rose, I just don't have anyone else to talk to. I don't really know anyone down here yet.'

'Eva, whatever you tell me won't go any further unless you want it to.'

'The thing is, I don't know where Dave was on the Sunday night that girl was raped. And there've been a couple of other occasions since when he hasn't said where he's been. I know it sounds crazy, he's a kind, gentle man, but that's how he is with me. You see, I know there've been cases when the closest people are the last to know.'

'You seriously think he has raped one girl, attacked another and killed a third?' Even though Rose had had her own suspicions she was shocked to hear Eva voice them.

'No. Not really.' But the doubt was there.

'I take it you have asked him?'

'Yes. He says he can't tell me. He was out last night, until very late. I pretended to be asleep, I couldn't go through that again, asking questions and not knowing the answer.'

Sunday. It was a Sunday that Lucy Chandler had been raped.

'And he said he was working during the day. He rarely does that, unless he's really behind because of the weather.'

'I understand your concern, Eva, but what do you expect me to do?'

'Nothing. I just wanted to tell someone, to see if it sounded as far-fetched to someone else. I just don't know what to do. Do you think I should tell the police? I'd have to do it anonymously, I couldn't bear for Dave to know even if he was guilty.'

'That must be your decision. Apart from his not telling you where he was, has anything else made you suspicious?'

She chewed the side of her thumbnail then took a sip of her wine. Rose thought she wasn't going to answer. 'He's got a plaster on his hand. He said he'd torn it on some barbed wire. The paper said the second girl bit her attacker on the hand. He hasn't taken the plaster off yet. Well, if he's changed it, it's not been when I've been around.'

'But he's working with earth, he can't afford to get dirt in the wound.'

'I've told myself that, too. Rose, please tell me, what should I do?'

All these things had crossed Rose's mind

before she had learnt of her mother's illness. She had not known what to do herself, how could she possibly advise Eva who obviously loved the man? 'Do you know someone called Rod Hill?'

'No.' Eva frowned. 'Wait, the name does ring a bell. I think Dave may have done some work for him. Why?'

'Oh, it isn't important. More wine?' She got up to pour it hoping Eva wouldn't question her further. 'Look, I think the police ought to know. I don't know Dave as you do, but I find it very hard to believe him capable of such things. On the other hand, as you said, you can't always judge. I know someone who would treat the situation sympathetically. Would you trust me to tell him? I won't even mention your name.'

'Yes. Yes, I think that's best. I can't live with this uncertainty. I love him, Rose, I'll still love him whatever he's done, but I couldn't live with him, protecting him, like some women do, knowing he'd hurt someone. There's been enough violence in my life.'

'All right, leave it to me. You don't think you might be in any danger, do you?'

'No. Strange as that sounds, I really don't.'

'Fine. I'll ring Dave if I do hear of a job.'

'Thank you.' Eva stood up. She was silhouetted

against the sunshine streaming through the kitchen door. She looked almost ethereal as she reached for her bag that was on the floor. 'Thank you for listening. I know I shouldn't have come, but there was no one else, and you were kind to me when I was here with Dave.' She smiled wanly. 'I could see you really wanted to be getting on with some work.'

'I'll be in touch, Eva.' Rose watched her walk down the drive. Now I'll really have to ring Jack, Rose thought.

Everyone connected with the three girls had been interviewed more than once but Inspector Jack Pearce was convinced that the person they were looking for did not know them. The girls had not known one another and there seemed to be no common denominator. It has to be the same person, Jack thought as he had packed up for the day on Monday. No weapon had been used. Lucy Chandler had received blows from a fist, as had Helen Trehearne, although not so many and she had managed to get away. Nichola Rolland had been manually strangled. Whoever it was did not go about armed. Not yet, at least. It was the *not yet* which worried Jack. Another murder must be prevented.

He thought about Laura as he drove home. Laura and Rose had known the identity of Lucy Chandler and neither of them had mentioned it to him. And Lucy Chandler was keeping something back, as was her boyfriend, Jason Evans. He had been interviewed early that morning.

'We went for a drive and stopped for a drink,' Jason had explained. 'We had a row, it started from nothing, and she walked out on me.'

'You didn't follow her?'

'No. I stayed in the pub for a while then I drove home.'

Hardly gallant, Jack had thought, but it wasn't a crime. The barmaid had confirmed his story up to the time he had left.

And Jason's description did not fit the very sketchy one he had been given by Helen Trehearne. Lucy had not been able to provide one at all. Why not? Too many questions. I'm going to forget it all for this evening and have a few pints myself, he decided.

He parked outside his flat and let himself in. It was stuffy. Being at street level he could not leave any windows open when he was out. He poured a beer and opened the back door. From the other side of the high fence separating him from his neighbour came the irritating buzz of a lawn-mower. The fragrance of newly cut grass was in the air. Jack stood still, his face to the sun, deciding which hostelry would have the benefit of his custom, when he was disturbed by the telephone. He went in to answer it.

'Hello, Jack. I'm glad I caught you. There's something, well, I think I need to talk to you.'

I bet you do, he thought, angry anew that she had not told him about her mother. She knew how much he liked and respected her parents. 'Oh?'

'Would it be convenient if I came over?'

'Yes, give me half an hour. I need a shower.' No point in saying no. He wanted, perhaps needed to hear what she had to say. And he wanted to see her far more than he wanted a solitary drink.

He heard the doorbell from the back garden where he had taken two chairs. It was too warm to sit indoors.

Rose stood on the doorstep clutching a bottle of wine, an anxious expression on her face. Without thinking, Jack bent to kiss her. She smelt of the perfume he had bought her and was wearing a dress. This must be serious. 'I was having a beer but we'll have the wine if you prefer?'

'I do.' She followed him into the house.

'Go and sit outside, I won't be a minute.' Having seen her he couldn't understand why he had felt so angry. She had that effect on him. 'Okay, what do you have to tell me?'

Rose took a deep breath. For a second she thought he knew about Tony. 'I've promised I wouldn't say how I found out, you'll have to respect that, Jack, but it seems that someone I know was missing on the night that Lucy was raped. Added to that, he has a plaster on his hand.'

She's gabbling, she doesn't want to be telling me this. And why is her face red? 'I see. Am I allowed to know the name of this person?'

Rose closed her eyes. She felt as if she was betraying both Dave and Eva. 'Dave Fox, my gardener.'

'Ah, the man about whom you managed to find out so much in such a short time.'

'Are you being sarcastic?' Rose felt angry, but she was aware her anger was misdirected. It was herself she was angry with for running to him with tales. But it was also the fact that, face to face with him she felt even more ashamed of what had taken place with Tony Boyd.

'No. So shall I go and pick him up?'

'I don't know what you should do, Jack. I just thought you ought to know.'

'Just like you thought I ought to know that you and Laura were aware of Lucy Chandler's identity and the fact that she had a boyfriend whose name you knew. It seems to me, Rose, that you only feel I ought to know things when it suits you.'

She stood and handed him her glass. 'I knew I shouldn't have come. It's always the same. I think I'm being helpful and you turn on me. I can't help it if people tell me things they won't tell you. It's no wonder, if you speak to them the way in which you speak to me.' Her eyes burned. I'm about to cry, she thought. How bloody ridiculous.

Jack saw the tears rise and cursed himself. He put his hand on her arm. 'There's no need for you to leave. At least drink the wine first. And tell me, Rose, how's Evelyn?'

And then she did cry. She had not realised how much emotion she had hidden from her friends and, especially, from her father. 'She's all right,' she finally said. 'They think she's over the worst. It was just such a shock. She's always been so fit and healthy, then suddenly, just like that she was in hospital. She looked so small in that bed, Jack. So small and vulnerable.'

He reached out and stroked her hair. 'It's okay. It sounds as if she'll pull through.'

'I know. But you should've seen Dad. He was pretending he'd be all right whatever happened but I could see what he was going through.'

He topped up her glass although she'd hardly touched her drink. Tonight there would be no more talk of work. Rose had come to him with information which may or may not be relevant. He would get someone else to deal with that. Now was the time to try to repair any rift between them. 'Have you eaten?' She shook her head. 'Then you have two choices, we can go out or you can chance my cooking?'

'I'm not very hungry.'

'You have to eat. Which is it to be?'

'Your cooking then.'

'I'll just see what delights the fridge reveals. You stay there.' He knew what there was to eat but he wanted to make that telephone call out of her hearing. 'I'm not sure of the best way of approaching this. Perhaps something along the lines that we know he works at various properties in the relevant areas and we wondered if he'd noticed any of these girls. Make sure he knows we're questioning everyone. If he's in the clear and thinks we've singled him out he'll have reason to complain. And find out if he's ever done any work for any of the girls' parents.'

Jack returned to the garden. He saw how tired Rose looked and realised the strain she had been under. He would do his best to cheer her up.

As the sun moved further westwards the garden became cooler. 'Let's go inside, supper won't be long.' Jack carried their glasses then set to in the kitchen.

'Sorry it wasn't very exciting,' he said as he piled the dirty dishes in the sink.

'It was fine.' The makeshift mixed grill had consisted of his breakfast ingredients: bacon, circles of herb flavoured local sausage cut from a ring, known as hog's pudding, eggs and mushrooms served with a tin of peas. 'I think I'll go home now, Jack. It's all beginning to catch up on me. I feel exhausted.'

'Want a taxi?'

'Yes, I think I do.'

Fifteen minutes later Rose paid the driver, let herself into the house and went straight to bed.

CHAPTER NINE

'What is it?' Joyce Jago studied her daughter's face.

'Nothing, Mum. Honestly.' Sam got up and left the kitchen where she and her mother had been sitting, a slice of toast untouched on her plate. There were only a few classes to attend until the end of term and they seemed so unnecessary now that the exams were over. It would be different this time next year when she would be awaiting the results of her A levels.

Upstairs she sat on the bed wondering what to do. It had been a mistake to offer to cover for Lucy, and the guilt at what had happened to her friend was eating away at her. And Lucy refused to speak to her, as if it really was Sam's fault. In the end she had admitted her part to the police but, out of loyalty to her friend, she had not given them Jason's name. 'Mum doesn't like Jason,' Lucy had told her. 'The only way I can get to see him is if I say I'm with you.' Sam had believed her at first but during one of their conversations Lucy had let things slip, things which, on their own didn't amount to much but which lately had worried Sam.

She got up and walked across the room to stare at herself in the mirror. Without vanity she realised that she was pretty. Her figure, in jeans and T-shirt, was slim with curves in the right places. Other girls, less attractive than her, had boyfriends, why didn't she? Lucy always accused her of being too serious, of thinking too much of the future while she wasted her youth. But Lucy had left school and had a job and Lucy had a boyfriend. Sam wanted more than that, she wanted a career, one that was respected and well paid. Perhaps boys her own age sensed that and left her alone. But it was Lucy who had been raped, Lucy who had not been with Jason at the end of the evening. And Sam thought she had an idea why that might be. Go to the police, her conscience dictated, but it might mean real trouble for Lucy and she couldn't put her through that now.

She picked up her knapsack, shoved her mobile phone in the bottom of it and left the house without knowing where she was going.

Joyce Jago heard the front door slam and sighed. Sometimes she wondered what life was all about. Her daughter lived in a world of her own and Ivan was away so often or off playing golf that she hardly seemed to have a family.

Sam had been questioned by the police but Joyce had not been present. Seventeen was considered old enough not to need an adult in attendance. Sam refused to discuss it with her but Joyce, once she had read the paper and coupled Lucy's lack of communication with Sam with the article, guessed at the truth. She shuddered to think it might have been her own daughter. If only Ivan wasn't away again she could have discussed it with him. The telephone was not the best mode of communication for a heart to heart.

But I do need to discuss this with someone, she thought, as she tilted Sam's plate over the waste-bin. The toast landed on top of the remains of the dinner Sam had left last night.

It was later that morning, as she sat in the secluded back garden of the spacious house Ivan's job had paid for, trying to capture on paper the mass of flowering clematis which trailed along the fence, that she wondered if Rose Trevelyan would lend a willing ear. She struck Joyce as a person who would be glad to help if it was possible. Joyce smiled at the irony of the situation. Rose was her tutor at the art classes she attended. They were both adults. Normally the situation was reversed and a troubled adolescent would go to her teacher with a problem, especially if it concerned her parents, not the other way around. The next class was tomorrow night but Joyce decided she couldn't wait any longer and, besides, she didn't want to discuss what was bothering her in front of the others. She got up, went back inside the house, looked up the number and rang it. There was no reply. Hesitating only a second or so she left a message asking Rose to ring her back. Feeling marginally relieved that she had done something she went back to complete the piece of work Rose had set for them. Natural life, she had said, adding no more, just smiling and allowing her pupils to make their own interpretation of the title. Joyce wondered if anyone would produce a nude and, if so, who they would have got to model for them.

* * *

'Hello.' Rose tried to smile but she was shocked at Lucy Chandler's appearance. Having only seen her once or twice her memory was of a plump, vivacious brunette who made up for average looks with an infectious smile and plenty of personality. From what Laura had told her Gwen had had problems controlling her, even as a small child. But this was no child. Lucy was seventeen and out at work. This was a young woman who might never trust a man again, who might never smile that wide-mouthed smile that Rose remembered.

Lucy nodded but did not respond verbally to Rose's greeting. Gwen Chandler sat at the table, pale but composed. 'Hello, Rose, Laura said you were coming.'

Rose sat down. Laura had introduced her to Gwen some time ago but Rose did not really know her any more than she knew the daughter. What do I say? Nice to see you again? Hardly, under the circumstances, and was she supposed to know what those circumstances were? Laura had not said when she telephoned.

'We've both taken another week off work. Lucy's in no state to go back yet,' Gwen said, making it clear that the subject was not taboo. 'How are you coping?'

'Not too well.'

Rose recalled that the husband had left when Lucy was small and, as far as she knew, only kept in touch with his daughter. Gwen, therefore, had to manage on her own. 'And you, Lucy?'

Lucy shrugged. Her thick, dark hair hung limply around her shoulders. It needed washing. 'Not much to cope with, is there? It's happened, nothing can change that.'

'And you've no idea who it was?' I shouldn't have said that, Rose thought. Straight in again, no tact.

'No. Don't you think I'd have named the bastard if I did?'

Anger, a good sign. Lucy was looking at Rose now. There was colour in her cheeks and a defiant expression on her face. Rose felt Laura's eyes on her own face. 'People don't always,' Rose said gently.

'You think I'm protecting someone? God, I'm sick of this whole thing. And if it wasn't for Jason . . .' she stopped and put her head in her hands.

Protecting Jason? From what? Rose wondered. 'Has he been to see you?'

'No. And I don't want him to. He won't want anything to do with me now.'

'I've tried to explain that it wasn't her fault, that she's nothing to feel guilty about, but she won't listen. Even the counsellor they sent couldn't get that through to her. No one deserves that to happen.' Gwen accepted the coffee Laura was handing around.

'How's your mum?' Laura decided no good would come of continuing the conversation.

'The same. Dad thinks they'll let her out on Saturday.' Rose wondered what she was doing there. None of them seemed willing to talk. 'That's a lovely watch,' she said as Lucy reached for her cup.

'Yes. It was a present.'

'Jason gave it to her. He's very generous. I wish you'd let me meet him, Lucy. I won't bite, you know.'

'It's too late now.'

Rose studied the interaction between mother and daughter. It was odd that the latter needed Sam to cover for her if Gwen had expressed a wish to meet Jason. Gwen was trying her best but Lucy's sullenness seemed contrived. It was an uncharitable thought after what the girl had been through.

'Can we talk about something else? I thought we were coming to see Laura to get us out of the house not to hold an inquisition.'

Rose was embarrassed. Lucy was right. The problem would not be solved by idle curiosity even if those asking the questions cared. 'I think I'd better be going. The weather looks as if it'll hold and I need to get some work done.' She stood and unhooked her bag from the back of the chair. It was worth one more go. 'Is there any message for Sam? I'll be seeing her mother tomorrow evening.'

'Yes. No. No, it doesn't matter.'

She needs her friend, Rose thought as she said goodbye, but she's too proud to admit it. Maybe I'll mention it to Joyce and leave it to her.

There was no breeze but even the still, warm air felt fresh after the claustrophobic atmosphere in Laura's kitchen. So much was not being said. Rose had done her bit, work must come first now. She had already decided not to go far, she would work from the beach. The painting had been planned in her head. Newlyn, with its steeply tiered houses, below them the harbour walls above which the masts of fishing vessels loomed and the sea in the foreground. The composition was perfect.

The sun moved imperceptibly across the bay, at first warming her shoulders then the side of her face. She worked solidly, unaware of the time which was passing. Finally Rose left the damp canvas on the easel and stood back to study her work, rubbing her stiff back with her hand. It was good. Another oil was well on its way to completion. She could have carried on a little longer but knew that the result of over-extension was staleness. Stop while the going's good, she told herself. Taking her flask from her bag she sat on the water-smoothed pebbles and thought how lucky she was. After David died she had not believed it possible to ever be happy again but she had come to appreciate loyal friends and her work and, more recently, a small claim to fame. There were so many people less fortunate than herself. Lucy Chandler for one. When the unfinished painting was dry enough to carry without danger of its smudging, Rose walked home.

Having unpacked her gear and cleaned her brushes she put everything in the larder then went to see if there had been any phone calls in her absence. The light blinked twice. Rose pressed the button and listened. 'It's Barry, Rose. Just a quick call to see how your mother's doing. Oh, and if you've got a minute, can I call in after work? If I don't hear from you I'll take it you're busy.'

The second message surprised her. It was from Joyce Jago, her most talented pupil. Few of them showed any great promise but as long as they enjoyed the classes and working on what they produced in their own time Rose did not see that it mattered. Joyce did not say what she wanted, only that she would be grateful if Rose could return the call. She glanced at her watch. Four-fifty. Joyce might well be at home; Rose had an idea that she worked part-time. She dialled the number given.

'Rose, thank you for ringing back. It sounds silly now but I really didn't know who else to talk to and my husband's away on business for a few more days.'

Rose waited. This was nothing to do with the evening class. What was expected of her now?

'It's about Sam really.'

I've been here once today, Rose thought, memories of the awkward morning returning. Lucy and now Sam. Again. Whatever made people think she was equipped to deal with teenage girls? 'Has something happened? Is she ill?'

'No. It's just the way she's been acting ever since the police came. Oh dear, I'll have to go now. I'm sorry, I really shouldn't have bothered you.'

'No, wait.' Rose had heard a door close in the background and guessed correctly that Sam had come home unexpectedly.

'I usually go for a walk about half-past five. Could you manage that?' Damn, I forgot about Barry, she thought. Whatever he wanted would now have to wait.

'Yes, I can. Shall I meet you somewhere?'

They agreed to be by the bandstand in Morrab Gardens at a quarter to six. Rose had time to change out of her paint-splattered clothes and ring her father before she set off. He was no longer spending every minute at the hospital, he had told her, it was tiring for him and for Evelyn. Satisfied that her mother's condition was improving and that June Potter, their neighbour, was keeping an eye on her father, Rose hung up.

She left the house grateful to be unencumbered by her canvas satchel or her photographic equipment. Walking briskly, enjoying her daily exercise, she reached Morrab Gardens with time to spare. Sitting on one of the seats by the bandstand she watched the birds flit between the trees and studied the sub-tropical plants, most of which were now in flower.

Joyce Jago arrived five minutes late, a little breathless from hurrying. She was a plump woman of about forty with permed blonde hair, a lived-in face and a careworn expression. Even so she was attractive although in a sensual rather than traditional way. 'Thanks for coming, Rose. I couldn't ask you to my place because I never know when Sam's going to be there.'

'I take it she's at the stage where communication with a parent isn't the done thing.' Rose wanted to keep it light. She crossed her legs and tugged at her short denim skirt when a man walking past lowered his eyes to her knees.

'I'm hoping that's just all it is. She's got the whole summer ahead of her now but, I don't know, she seems depressed.'

'Boyfriend trouble?'

'Not that I'm aware of. She's never mentioned anyone in particular and she's stopped going out with her friends in the evenings. She just sits up in her room playing music.' Joyce smiled ruefully. 'I can't even complain that it's loud.'

It has to be to do with Lucy, Rose realised. Lucy was hiding something, maybe Sam had something to hide, too. Did they know the man who had raped and killed? If so, no wonder Sam was depressed. But there was no way she could ask. Joyce might not even know what had happened to Lucy.

'I don't know why I'm here, really. I suppose I just wanted to unburden myself.'

But her face said it all, she was afraid that Sam was in some sort of serious trouble, but Rose had no idea what she could do to help.

They sat in the sunshine surrounded by trees and plants and their shadows which lengthened over the lawns. After a couple of minutes Joyce spoke again. 'I think her best friend was raped. Sam was supposed to be meeting her. I think she somehow blames herself.'

So much guilt, Rose thought. So much unnecessary guilt.

'They've been friends for as long as I can remember. Sam's hurt because Lucy won't speak to her.'

'Why not?'

'I don't know. Lucy probably doesn't feel like speaking to anyone at the moment. Although it did cross my mind that the two of them might have been involved in something else. But there's no point in asking, Sam won't tell me anything.

'I'm sorry, Rose. It's just so unhappy in that house at the moment. I'll be glad when Ivan gets back. Anyway, thanks for listening, I appreciate it.'

They parted at the park gates. Joyce said she

would be at the class the following evening. 'I wouldn't miss it for anything, it helps to keep me sane,' she added with a wan smile.

Rose made her way home thinking that she more than deserved her glass of wine.

There was a tuna steak she could grill and some salad. That was as much effort as she was prepared to make that evening. With a glass of Rioja and a cigarette to hand she rang Barry, apologised for not returning his call sooner and arranged to meet him the following night. As the tuna was cooking slowly in the oven she got out a pen and paper and made a diagram. Each encircled name could be linked to another: herself, Jack, Barry, Daphne and Rod Hill, Dave Fox and Eva Fenton, Joyce and Sam Jago, Gwen and Lucy Chandler and Laura. They were all connected in some small way. She knew nothing of the other two girls, only that Doreen Clarke knew Helen Trehearne because she lived nearby and Nichola Rolland because she had once done some spring-cleaning for her mother when she still lived locally. When they moved to Liskeard, Nichola had remained in the area, living in a one-bedroomed flat until she finished her schooling. Doreen's name was added to the list.

Later, just before she fell asleep, a strange

idea came into Rose's head. She put it down to tiredness.

Just after two a.m. a noise woke her. It was probably a gull on the roof, but even so she went downstairs to check that the doors were locked and the windows closed. With so many odd things going on she could not afford to take chances.

CHAPTER TEN

Inspector Jack Pearce sat at his desk cursing modern science. Progress in forensic detection may have escalated considerably but in this instance it had proved useless. Lucy Chandler's bruising had been photographed and her clothes taken away for analysis but the results proved nothing. Stray hairs and fibres could have come from anywhere. If Helen Trehearne had scratched instead of bitten her attacker there might have been skin under her fingernails and if Nichola Rolland had not been murdered amongst the Towans more evidence might have been collectable from the ground. As it was the sand held no footprints, no signs of a struggle, no nothing. An overnight breeze had shifted the particles. They had a small collection of cigarette ends and litter which might have been there since last summer. That was the extent of their findings.

Frustrated, he went over the conversation he had had with one of his officers. Dave Fox and Eva Fenton had been eating when two uniformed men knocked at the door of the caravan the previous night. It had been easy enough to find; they had simply asked in the village. 'She was far more worried than him, sir,' PC Roberts had told him. 'Anyway he agreed to answer our questions and she took herself off for a walk.'

Jack had worked out that Rose's source of information concerning Dave Fox must have been Eva herself. And if the man's partner was worried that certainly gave cause for concern.

But Fox's alibi had been checked. It was more than likely he was in the clear. More than likely, but not certain. There were a few more questions to ask and a few more people to interview. By the end of the day he should have some more answers. And then he would find out what Rose was up to.

Having worked until late Jack went straight home but decided it was too late to disturb Rose with a telephone call. He felt restless, through tiredness, and vaguely puzzled. Over two weeks had passed since Lucy Chandler had been raped. In all that time there had been no more burglaries or attempted burglaries other than a couple they had detected which, no matter how hard they had tried, could not be related to the previous unsolved ones. They've moved on, he decided. It was as we thought, some gang from outside the area. They would now become someone else's problem.

He made some toast and a pot of tea then fell asleep in an armchair before he had drunk it.

'You have to talk to me,' Eva said on Wednesday morning as she stood in the doorway of the caravan. When the police arrived she had left, unable to bear the thought of Dave being questioned even though she wanted to know the truth herself. For almost two hours she had wandered along country lanes hardly noticing the flowers now filling the hedgerows or the peaceful beauty of her surroundings. When she returned, Dave was alone. He had cleared the table and washed up. They went to bed having hardly exchanged a word but in the night Eva felt Dave's arm around her.

'What is it you want to know?'

'Why the police were here.'

'I think you know that already, Eva.'

She gasped. He had guessed her part in it.

'Why did you do it?'

'I didn't do anything, Dave. Honestly. You wouldn't tell me where you were, I was worried sick you were in trouble of some sort. I confided in someone, that's all.'

'Then why did they come here? How did they know I was here?'

'Does it matter if you haven't done anything? Dave, please. Just tell me where you were those times. I love you, I need to be able to trust you.'

So he told her. Eva listened, initially with disbelief and then, when the truth sunk in she knew she had been close to losing the most important thing in her life. Her distrust of the man she loved could easily have driven him away from her.

Rose looked out of her bedroom window and shook her head in mock disbelief. The weather was becoming even more unpredictable. Unless it cleared up quickly she would have no option other than to stay at home and work.

Once a few bits of housework were out of the way and she had eaten some breakfast it was obvious that the rain was not going to stop. Rose went up to the attic and began to work.

During a short break she stood in the recess of the sitting-room window, drinking coffee, just able to make out the outline of a large vessel which was coming into view. What will my class have produced? she wondered, smiling at the ideas which came into her mind. Natural Life had been the title she had given them, not even sure herself what she meant. It wasn't such a bad thing, maybe she had been too pedantic in setting the type of work they were expected to complete in their own time. Perhaps it was better to allow them to express themselves freely. Whatever they produced would give her some insight into their personalities.

The early afternoon was spent sorting out her income tax returns. She had mastered self-assessment but the forms needed to be in by September. It was such a nuisance when all she wanted to do was to paint. At four thirty she opened the larder door and glowered at the basket of clothes waiting to be ironed. It would be easier to do it now than leave it until the creases had dried further. She got out the iron and board and switched on the radio. The telephone had remained silent all day.

At eight o'clock, halfway through her class, Rose said, 'All right, let me see what you've done this evening then I'll have a look at what you've achieved at home.' The students had been asked to plan a landscape, not to draw or paint one, simply to mark where objects might be placed in order to produce a balanced picture. There were several reasonable attempts.

Natural Life covered a lot of ground. The elderly pensioner who kept to himself and came and went in a taxi had produced a graphic, albeit inaccurate, representation of a fox slaughtering a chicken. Both creatures were in the centre of the page and they were ringed by blood and feathers. Flowers were predominant, Joyce's clematis being by far the best. There was a fair attempt at a seascape and one humorous attempt at a cartoon where three plump children sat in front of a television screen eating burgers, bottles of cola at their sides. Rose smiled. Yes, that was natural life for many children nowadays. She commented on each, offering encouragement rather than criticism, surprised that there wasn't one attempt at a nude amongst the lot.

At five past nine as she saw the last of them out Joyce waited by her side. 'I just wanted to thank you again for yesterday.'

'Forget it. I'll see you next week.'

As she locked up she saw Barry walking up the hill towards her. I'm going to forget everything and have a quiet, enjoyable drink with a friend, she decided. And that friend although obviously worried about something, looked pleased to see her.

'Hi, Barry. Where're we going?'

'Now it's finally stopped raining I thought we could walk back to Newlyn and have a drink there.'

The weather had improved although there were purple tinges on the horizon promising an early dusk and possibly more rain during the night. 'I'm glad to hear it. I didn't really feel like straying too far from home.'

'I've got the hint, my dear. You want a reasonably early night.'

Barry took her arm as they went down the hill. Rose tried not to mind but she always felt awkward being tactile in public. She grinned. Except at times with Jack when, looking at his strong, handsome profile, she had an urge to kiss him. Not that she would ever let him know that. The grin faded as she thought of Tony Boyd. 'You've got paint on your fingers.'

'Yes. I've started decorating. Only the undercoat

but the place looks better already. Once it's finished and you've helped me choose the furniture I shall throw a party.'

'A party?'

'Well, you and me and Laura and Trevor. Maybe even Doreen and Cyril.'

Rose smiled. That was as much of a party as Barry was ever likely to throw.

They reached the Promenade. Some small boats were close to the shore; lone fishermen in dinghies and others enjoying the solitary exercise of rowing. Further out were a few blue sailed yachts. The weather and tides had been right for fishing so there wasn't a trawler in sight and only a few masts to be seen beyond the wall of Newlyn Harbour. One or two of the strings of white bulbs lining the sea-front came on. For some reason they never worked in unison and some would go off again at random. They had been like that for several years.

'If I'd known it was going to be this busy I'd have kept the shop open,' Barry muttered as they passed people who had ventured out for an evening walk now that the rain had stopped.

'What ever for? You make enough money. And the whole idea of employing Daphne was to ensure you got some time to yourself.' Barry flinched, reminding Rose that he had said he needed to talk to her. 'Is Daphne a sore point?'

'No, of course not. We get on really well. She's worried, that's all.'

'Who isn't at the moment? So do tell.'

Barry related most of the conversation which had taken place between them in the shop during a quiet period. Daphne, knowing what had happened to the three girls, had been terrified that Rod would come under suspicion. 'They'll be investigating anyone with something like that in their past,' she had confided. 'I just don't know what it'll do to him, Barry. And if I was asked I couldn't say where he was on those occasions. I don't suppose he'd remember himself either.'

'But surely the police would've paid him a visit already?' Rose said as they neared the art gallery.

'That's what I told Daphne but she says it's only a matter of time and then their problems will all start again. I suggested he had a word with Jack, admitted the reasons for moving down here rather than wait for the police to go to him.'

'That was a bit rash.'

'Was it?' Barry thumbed his glasses into place. He had thought it a good idea. 'Anyway, she said she'll discuss it with him and let me know what they decide.'

What on earth will Jack think about Barry and I taking matters into our own hands? she wondered as they rounded the corner and crossed the bridge. Rose thought it best to let the matter drop and wait to learn more from Jack.

The Swordfish was quiet, as the Newlyn pubs often were when most of the fleet was at sea. Even so it took several minutes for Rose and Barry to reach the bar because they stopped to exchange a few words with people they knew who were already drinking.

Forty minutes later Barry walked her home. Food and bed were now her priorities.

On Thursday Rose took advantage of the reappearance of the sun and went down to the beach. One more session and the Newlyn piece would be finished. She worked from above the tideline, as she had done before. A herring-gull landed and, head on one side, watched her until it realised there was no food to be had. It flew off, screeching, its wings creating a draft as it clumsily gained height.

It remained warm and sunny until the early afternoon when white clouds drifted slowly from the north and altered the light. Rose packed up and went home. Jack had left a message asking her to call him back. Before she could do so Doreen rang. 'How's your mum doing?'

'She's fine. Improving all the time. It won't be long before she's home.'

'I'm pleased to hear it. Anyway, can you come over on Saturday night? It's Cyril's birthday and I thought I'd surprise him.'

'Yes, I'd love to.' First Barry, now Doreen. What was happening to her friends? Her social life was becoming hectic. And she'd have to think of a suitable present. 'What time?'

'Half-sixish. We don't keep late hours.'

'I'll bring a bottle.'

'You can bring a guest, too. Jack, or Barry. There'll only be a few of us, nothing special, like.'

'I went to see John and Sheila Rolland yesterday afternoon. Being a Wednesday it was the first chance I'd got. I didn't know if they'd want any company but I couldn't not go.'

The murdered girl's parents. Doreen had mentioned that she knew them.

'It's so sad. They only moved up to Liskeard about eight months ago. I think I told you that Nicky was expected to go to college later this year and they'd all agreed she'd finish her schooling here. Sheila says she wonders what it was all for now and that it would've been better for Nichola not to have had an education if it could have prevented her death. Anyway, I'm glad I went, I'd hate for them to think no one cares. I won't keep you, maid, I know you'm always busy. I'll see you on Saturday.'

Rose hung up and dialled Jack's Camborne number. He answered immediately.

'Ah, at last. You never seem to be in lately.'

'Don't moan. I've been taking advantage of the weather every opportunity I can get. It's so damn changeable.'

'I expect you're busy tonight.'

'No. I was hoping for a quiet evening.'

'Oh.'

'Why do you ask?'

'No special reason. Just some companionable conversation.'

By the tone of his voice Rose thought that highly unlikely. 'Look, if you can get here early we can have a chat, if that's what you want. I'm still catching up on sleep.' It was true. Since her mother's illness her nights had been disturbed.

'Fine. I'll get away early and be there as soon as I can.'

With all that had happened since, Bristol seemed in the far distance now. Rose longed to go somewhere different, to find a change of scene and forget everything except painting, but she knew that luxury would have to wait until she was certain her mother's health was completely restored.

The clouds had drifted out to sea and the sun was shining again. Rose picked up the book she was reading and went to sit in the garden. Engrossed in the plot, she did not notice Jack's car until it had turned into the drive.

'I left as soon as I could,' he said as he got out and shut the car door. 'God, I'm shattered.'

Rose could have guessed that. He looked tired and hot and his shirt was rumpled, which was unusual as he took care of the way he dressed. 'Then you'd better join me in a drink.' She went inside and fetched another glass.

'Thanks.' Jack took off his jacket and sat on the bench then stared silently out over the bay.

'Jack, what is it?' Rose asked when she returned. It was unlike him not to initiate the conversation.

'Look, I know this won't go any further, but I'd still like you to promise to keep what I'm about to tell you to yourself.'

'Of course I will. You have my word.'

'It looks like Dave Fox is in the clear.'

'I'm so glad.'

'But the thing is, we've still got no other suspects.'

Rose didn't know what to say. She just hoped her interference hadn't destroyed the relationship between Dave and Eva even if it had helped to prove his innocence.

'There's something else. God, Rose, I really wish you lived in isolation at times.'

'What's that supposed to mean?'

'Rod Hill, that's what it means. How come you know the only two men we've had the slightest reason to suspect?'

'Because, as you well know, Jack this is a very small community and I do not live in isolation. I needed a gardener, Doreen recommended Dave, and, I hope you remember, it was Barry who introduced me to the Hills. Go and vent your temper on him for a change. Anyway, what about Rod Hill?'

'I apologise. I just don't know what to think any more. I'm so bloody tired.' He ran a hand through his thick springy hair and sighed. 'Rod Hill has a past. Okay, any charges were dropped but the girl was fifteen. And you, Rose, knew that.'

'How do you know?'

'I spoke to the Hills. Daphne said she confided

in Barry and he, in turn, told you, and you were also both at the house one evening. Barry admitted that much.'

'You've spoken to Barry?'

'Well, don't sound so surprised. I've got to speak to anyone and everyone connected with this.'

'And?'

'And Rod Hill can't recall where he was on the last two occasions, only that he was at the pub on the Sunday night of the first rape. We're now questioning witnesses.'

Poor Rod and Daphne. It will all start again for them, she thought. But Rose understood how Jack must feel, his anger wasn't really personal. But ought she to mention her suspicions regarding Lucy? No, that could wait. She'd have a word with Laura first. 'Stay for supper, Jack. Don't go back to your empty flat.' She took his hand but he did not respond.

He sighed again and tried to smile. 'Thanks. I couldn't face cooking tonight and I've eaten too many takeaways recently.'

'You sit there and have another drink while I see to the food.'

Through the kitchen window she could see him sitting without drinking, gazing across at

St Michael's Mount although it was doubtful he was actually seeing it. He's really worried, she thought, and I don't think anything I can do will make the slightest difference.

But Rose was wrong. After they'd eaten and taken their coffee into the sitting-room he began to discuss his worries. The feeling was the same amongst all his colleagues, they suspected they might never find Nichola Rolland's killer. 'It's the frustration,' he repeated, 'it makes it so much harder to concentrate on anything else. And I keep thinking there must be something vital we've overlooked.'

Rose had no answer to that. All she could do was to pour him more coffee and listen. Her own concerns seemed unimportant in contrast. She kept them to herself.

'Stay the night,' she said later, hating to see him so dejected.

Jack nodded and followed her upstairs. In bed he lay with his arm curled around her and finally fell asleep. Rose smiled before falling asleep herself. They had not made love but it didn't matter. Something had changed in their relationship. For once she had been the one to offer comfort and Jack had accepted it. And she was glad they hadn't made love, she still felt guilty about Tony, guilty and ashamed. It had been an unintentional one-night stand on her part, but Tony must have felt the same because, despite what he'd said, he hadn't rung her after all.

Jack left early without waking Rose. She opened her eyes surprised to see his side of the bed empty. Downstairs she found a short note thanking her for the meal and the bed. He had left by the front door which locked itself on the latch when closed. *I'll ring you*, the note concluded, followed by his name and a kiss.

Rose took herself down to the beach to complete her view of Newlyn. Friday. The start of the weekend and it promised to be hot. There were more people around now and it was difficult not to be distracted by those who stopped to watch her work. Needing a break she lay down, shielded her eyes from the sun with her forearm and half dozed as she listened to the cries of the gulls and the muted sound of voices as people walked along the path above her.

When she stood she felt dizzy from the heat. The oils had dried. Rose stepped back. Yes, it was good. She would see if Geoff Carter was willing to display it in his gallery.

As she was almost passing Laura's house Rose

rang the bell hoping for a cup of tea and some gossip before she went home.

'You're in luck, I've just made a pot. I've been sitting on the back step soaking up the sun.'

'I can tell. Your face is red.'

'Come and join me.'

Rose did so. It was very warm but the sun's rays were no longer penetrating the narrow alley at the back of Laura's house. 'I wanted to ask you about Jason, Lucy's boyfriend. Do you know him?'

'No. Never met him. Why?'

'He's unemployed, isn't he?'

'I believe so.'

'Then how can he afford to give Lucy expensive presents? Did you see that watch she was wearing?'

Laura shrugged her thin shoulders. 'Don't ask me. Perhaps his parents help him out.'

'Maybe. And another thing, Gwen seemed keen to meet him yet Sam told me she didn't approve of Lucy seeing him on the quiet.'

'Honestly, Rose, you see mysteries everywhere.'

'Well, think about it. If it isn't a mystery someone is lying and I can't believe it's Gwen.'

'If you think Jason's guilty of something tell Jack. You drive us all nuts at times, Rose

Trevelyan. Now, are you staying for supper or going home to sulk?'

Rose grinned. Laura always managed to put things back in perspective. 'Going home. I'm too old for all this socialising.' She felt herself blush. It was not Cyril's birthday or Barry mentioning a party which came into her mind, but the evening she had spent with Tony.

Laura raised an eyebrow. 'Tell me his name?'

'What?'

'You heard me. There's a man involved, I can see by your face.'

'Don't ever tell a soul,' Rose said when she had finished her confession. 'Especially not Jack.'

'There you are, I was right.'

'What do you mean?'

'You care about Jack far more than you think, that's why you don't want to hurt him. Anyway, you can trust Aunty Laura. Run along home now and indulge your guilt. I'll see you soon.' Rose stopped at the Co-op to buy some wine to take to Doreen's then, crossing the road, she went into the newsagent's to buy a card for Cyril. She had already decided to give him a small watercolour of the Hayle estuary she had painted more for pleasure than commercial reasons.

She was rummaging in a kitchen drawer for

a biro with which to sign Cyril's card when she came across the list she had written on a piece of scrap paper which connected many people she knew. She studied it carefully.

Name:	Knows:
Me:	Jack, Joyce & Sam Jago, Dave Fox & Eva Fenton, Rod & Daphne Hill, Doreen, Gwen & Lucy Chandler, Laura.
Jack:	Whole investigation. Will probably speak to them all eventually.
Barry:	Me, Rod & Daphne, Laura, Doreen, (met Dave & Eva at fête), Jack.
Rod & Daphne:	Barry, Dave Fox, Me
Laura:	Gwen & Lucy, Me, Jack, Barry, Doreen, (not sure if she's met Joyce Jago.)
Doreen:	Dave & Eva, Me, Barry, Jack, Helen Trehearne, Nichola Rolland and her parents.

Has Jack looked at it in this way? she wondered. If not, he ought to because there were far too many connections for comfort.

CHAPTER ELEVEN

Jason Evans had had plenty of girlfriends, most of whom he tired of quickly. He had been surprised when Lucy Chandler had ditched him, since that was usually his prerogative. He had not known her reasons at the time, had not, in fact, known until the police had picked him up. When they asked where he had been on Sunday evening it became obvious that they were questioning him about the rape he had heard of. He had not been able to help them. He and Lucy had gone for a drive, stopped for a drink and ended up arguing. She'd walked off and left him and he'd left some time afterwards. Only later, when she refused to take or return his calls did he realise that Lucy might have been the girl they were talking about.

He wasn't sure how he felt about what had happened to her. Deep down was some illogical belief that nice girls didn't get raped. Consciously he was aware that this was unfair and ridiculous. After ten days when she still refused to return the messages he left on her mobile phone he put her out of his mind. And now there was Liz.

Liz and another girl had been buying drinks at the bar in a club on Wednesday evening. It was stifling, but in a strappy dress with her long blonde hair loose around her shoulders she had looked cool and in control. Jason and his friend had paid for their drinks.

'I'm here on holiday,' Liz had told him. 'I'm staying with my grandparents. They're okay,' she had added seeing the surprise on his face. 'I come down most summers, so does Kate. We take the same two weeks off work and the grandparents put us up so that we can afford to go abroad once a year as well.'

Shrewd as well as pretty, Jason thought. He had taken her out for the day on Thursday, grateful that his friend had hit it off with Kate and had made similar arrangements.

'Don't your grandparents mind your being out all the time?' he asked when he took her home.

'No. They're happy to see us, of course, but they have different interests and they're out most of the time themselves when the weather's good.'

'Can I see you tomorrow?'

'Yes, but not until the evening. Kate and I are going shopping in Truro then we're treating my grandparents to lunch.'

'You're all going?'

Liz had smiled. 'No, I don't think that would appeal to them. They're visiting some friends in Redruth and meeting us later. We probably won't get back until late because they want to stop at a garden centre. We're going over by train and coming back with them in the car. I'll meet you at seven-thirty.'

It was a shame. He had hoped to take her back to his bedsit but there was still time – there were another eleven days of her holiday left. Instead, he walked her home.

On Friday morning Dave Fox set off for work. It was going to be a hot day and he wanted to get started early. Mr and Mrs Johnson were a pleasant couple to work for. Throughout the summer he cut their grass and tidied the flower-beds on a fortnightly basis. Every so often he put down lawn weedkiller and trimmed the hedges.

In the late autumn he dug the ground and planted bulbs. The Johnsons left him to it and paid him for however many hours he'd worked without question, even though they were not always present.

They were leaving the bungalow as he arrived. 'It won't take long today,' Dave told them. He'd mow the lawns but the flowers were now so abundant that there was little room to weed between them.

'Shall I pay you now?' Mrs Johnson asked.

'No. Leave it until next time. I might only be an hour.'

They got into their car and drove off. Dave got out the mower and got to work.

He had finished the back and was starting on the front when he heard voices. He had been unaware there was anyone else in the house. He looked up. Two girls in short skirts and summer tops were coming down the path.

'Hello,' one of them said.

'Hello.' They looked vaguely familiar, he had probably seen them there before.

By the time they had disappeared from sight he had forgotten them.

The work took longer than he had expected or else he had been slower because he was hot.

Just before eleven he packed his tools in the van then sat in the shade to drink the tea in his flask. Things were all right between him and Eva now. He had been shocked when the police had questioned him but he could understand their reasons for doing so. That was now in the past, all he wanted was a future with Eva. He screwed the cup back onto the flask and got up. It was time to leave for his next job.

Rose cursed when the telephone rang but she had rarely been able to let the answering-machine take over if she was in the house. It took several seconds before she recognised the panic-stricken voice gabbling down the line.

'Calm down, Eva, I can't understand you.'

'It's Dave. The police've come for him again. Oh, Rose, I can't stand it. He didn't do it, I know he didn't.'

'Where are you?'

'In a phone box.'

'I mean, shall I pick you up?' Rose sighed. This was not the quiet evening she had hoped for.

'Would you? I've got nowhere else to turn.'

'Tell me exactly where you are and stay there. I'll be with you as soon as I can.'

Within minutes she was on her way and

within twenty minutes Eva was sitting in the passenger seat, pale but calmer. Rose drove to the nearest pub. 'Come on, you look like you need a drink.'

The village pub was low-ceilinged with original beams and a flagstone floor. It was pleasantly cool after the heat of the day, and seemingly dark but their eyes soon adjusted. Even in July a faint smell of woodsmoke from the unlit fire still lingered. They chose a table inside as the garden was crowded and they didn't want their conversation to be overheard.

'What's this all about, Eva?'

'I don't know. Dave got home quite early and we were thinking about walking in to Hayle when the police arrived. They wanted to know where I'd been and I said I'd done some shopping and been at the caravan until they arrived. Then they asked Dave if he'd mind going with them to make a statement. They also said they wanted to take his fingerprints.

'The thing is, Rose, he was working for the Johnsons this morning.'

'The Johnsons?' Rose was confused, the name meant nothing. She had imagined it was to do with the murder.

'Their bungalow was broken into. They were

out at the time. Dave saw them leave. Then a little while later the girls left.'

'Which girls, Eva? You're not making much sense.'

'One's the Johnsons' granddaughter, Liz, the other one is her friend.'

'So Dave was there on his own.'

'Yes. He's worked for them for some time, they wouldn't have left him on his own if they didn't trust him.'

'There's not much we can do but wait,' Rose said. 'Obviously they have to question him if he was left alone at the property.'

'It's worse than that. You see, Dave can remember exactly what time he left because he needed to know how long he'd worked so the Johnsons could pay him but an elderly neighbour said she thought she'd heard breaking glass about the time Dave said he'd left.'

Rose sipped the bitter shandy she had ordered because she was driving. It was hard to imagine Dave Fox breaking a window and entering someone's home, especially the home of people who trusted him. 'Was much taken?'

'They didn't say.'

'Did they search the van or the caravan?'

'No.'

'Well, that's a hopeful sign.' Unless they didn't have time to get a warrant, she realised. 'These girls, does he know anything about them?'

'No. Why?'

'I just wondered. Look, Eva, if they release Dave, get him to speak to the Johnsons. Well, I expect he'll have to anyway, one way or another. See if he can find out anything about the granddaughter and her friend.' Rose wondered if the same thought had crossed Jack's mind but it would not be easy to find out without antagonising him. He was bound to accuse her of fantasising. 'Let me drive you back. Dave could turn up at any time.'

Rose pulled into a gateway to let Eva out. 'Where do the Johnsons live?'

Eva told her. It was a Penzance address, although the bungalow was on the outskirts and quite secluded.

'And that other thing, those girls. I should never have doubted him, Rose. Do you know where he was? He was doing up a place for me. It's an old barn, not one of your conversions, but really falling down. No roof or windows. He's used what money he brought from Derbyshire and he lives so simply he was able to buy it outright. There was already planning permission granted to convert it into living accommodation and that's what he'd started doing. He didn't want me to see it until it looked more like a building than a heap of rubble.'

Rose could believe it was the sort of thing Dave would do. 'Try not to worry,' she said before she left. Her mind was full of ideas and tomorrow, somehow or other, she would convey them to Jack.

Even though some of his fingerprints had been found on doors and windows of the bungalow, Dave Fox was released. Mr Johnson confirmed that Dave had made minor repairs to the locks and occasionally did inside work if they required it. He had spoken up for Dave, it was Liz who had said that he was alone there after she and Kate had left and along with the shaky evidence of the neighbour it had been enough to cast suspicion on him. Apart from which the name was already familiar to the police and they were aware that there were two teenage girls staying at the bungalow.

'They didn't tell me what, if anything, had been taken,' he told Eva when, white-faced, they sat either side of the tiny table in the caravan and shared a bottle of cider. 'I can't believe what's happening. As far as I know I've never committed a crime in my life. It's as if someone, or fate, has got it in for me.'

Eva reached for his hand. 'I should never have doubted you,' she said. 'Will you ever be able to forgive me?'

'Of course. I can see how it must've looked but I didn't want to spoil the surprise.'

'It's a lovely surprise, Dave. The next problem is the question of my finding a job.'

'Keep looking, something's bound to turn up in the end.'

'Maybe. But I think I ought to try for office or shop work.'

'No. Never. Never do anything you don't want to, Eva, that's where I went wrong. We're all right, we've enough money to keep us. You'll know when the right thing comes along. Now let's cheer up.'

They finished the cider and got into bed. Lying with her arms around him, Eva told Dave she had been to see Rose Trevelyan. 'I wish I could be like her. She seems so sensible and she's doing a job she really loves; you can tell by the way she talks about her work. And she can please herself when she works, and all that time spent out of doors, it must be wonderful.'

'But she probably had some money behind her when she started, Eva. Very few artists make enough to live on. She's a widow, I expect there were pensions or insurance policies. Please don't worry, something will turn up.'

Eva sighed. If only she had a talent like that. She was too tired and too relieved to think about it further. She closed her eyes and waited for sleep.

Lucy Chandler had been persuaded to join some friends for a drink on Friday evening. 'I don't want to go,' she told her mother. 'I know it's stupid but I keep thinking he's out there waiting for me.'

Gwen feared the same although it was irrational, unless, of course, Lucy did know who it was. 'You'll be with people you know, just make sure you stick with them. And, whatever you do, get a taxi home. And Lucy, don't you think it's time you rang Sam?'

Lucy nodded. She felt bad about that but had been too ashamed on two counts to face her. 'I'll do it in the morning. She'll probably be out herself on a Friday night.'

Gwen left it at that. It was enough that Lucy was going out. She had not left the house without her mother since the awful night of the rape. Gwen had decided that she must return to work on Monday, that things had to seem normal even if they weren't.

Lucy's friends had arranged to call for her. There were two of them. Neither questioned her on her absence from work or social events which led her to believe that they must have guessed the truth, and she was grateful for their silence. She was shaking by the time they reached the Longboat, a pub at the bottom of the town. It was crowded and noisy, the music making it hard to be heard. Getting there at all had been an effort and she knew she could not face going on to a club later. But she decided to stick it out for a while.

As they made their way to the end of the bar where there was more space, Lucy saw Jason huddled in a corner with a girl she didn't know. His arm was across her shoulders, his face was close to hers as he said something. Lucy realised she was not jealous but pleased. Jason Evans was a thing of the past. One of her friends who had known him since schooldays had seen him and went over to say hello.

Rose watched the dusk follow the setting sun over the bay. Lights came on around the coastline and the large ship anchored in the bay was lit up like a cruise liner. How can such awful things happen in such a beautiful place, she asked herself. And how come so many people I know seem caught up in this nastiness? Dave and Eva, trying to begin a new life, had already had two setbacks. She hoped they would survive them. Rod and Daphne, also trying for a new start, were not being given the chance to leave the past behind them. Perhaps no one could ever escape it. I haven't, she realised, David will always be a part of me no matter where I go or what I do. He helped to make me what I am.

Feeling slightly melancholy, she put on a CD. Lively trad jazz came loudly through the speakers. She switched on the table lamps and went to pour a glass of wine. Tomorrow was Cyril's birthday. Rose suddenly remembered that she hadn't invited anyone to go with her, not that it mattered, she was quite happy to go alone. It wasn't much after ten, not too late to ring Barry, but there was no answer. She tried Jack's number. He was at home. 'I know it's short notice,' she began before offering the invitation.

'I could do with a change of scene. What time does it start?'

'Early. Half six. You know Cyril and Doreen, they're up before sunrise.'

'Were you thinking of driving?'

'Not really. We can get the bus over and a taxi home.' Few trains stopped at Hayle.

They arranged a time to meet but before Jack could hang up, Rose asked what had happened to Dave Fox.

'How did you know we questioned him?'

'I saw Eva.'

There was a few seconds silence. 'Look, Rose, I'd rather, oh, blast it.' He could hardly tell her who she could socialise with. And this time he was sure she wasn't in danger, the man they were looking for liked teenage girls. He knew she wouldn't stop asking questions, it was the way she was made and if he said as much she would become more stubborn than ever. 'We've let him go. For the moment. It's just too much of a coincidence that he's been involved, however obliquely, in two investigations.'

'Jack, I . . .' but Rose thought better of voicing her suspicions of Lucy Chandler over the telephone. What she had to say could wait. Jack finding Nichola Rolland's killer was far more important.

'Rose?'

'It's nothing. I'll see you tomorrow.' She sat down to finish her glass of wine and picked up a new library book from the pile. Underneath was one she had finished. She frowned, trying to recall what it was about the plot that had set her thinking. It can't have been important, she decided as she opened a biography of Charlotte Brontë. But whatever it was kept niggling at the back of her mind and prevented her from concentrating on what she was reading. She went to find the list of names. Once more she studied it. Something was wrong, something didn't quite fit, but she just couldn't decide what it was.

Doreen Clarke went off to do her Saturday morning shopping wearing a plain cotton skirt and blouse. She had never taken to wearing jeans or trousers which would not have flattered her dumpy shape, not even for work. She would be home in plenty of time to prepare some snacks and shower and change. Cyril would spend the day in the garden, leaving it until the last minute before showering.

At six o'clock all was ready. Doreen looked with pleasure at the plates of food set out in the kitchen and the bowls of flowers in the living-room, flowers which Cyril had chosen carefully. The scent of roses filled the room.

It had been a muggy start to the day. The mist, thick enough to wet the skin, had hung low and heavy until mid-morning when the pale lemon globe of the sun had shown thinly through the moisture and fingers of sunlight had penetrated its layers. Now the sky was a clear blue. Doreen stood in the kitchen doorway enjoying the earthy smell of the garden and the piquancy of the tomato plants which Cyril had just watered. She had changed into a summer dress of pale blue cotton with sprigs of pink flowers. It suited her, enhancing her clear complexion and bringing out the blueness of her eyes. A car stopped outside. She heard voices and realised the first of her guests had arrived. She walked down the side of the bungalow to the front.

'Good to see 'e, maid,' she said, kissing Rose on the cheek. Beside her stood the tall, handsome Inspector Pearce who Doreen hoped would marry her friend one day. 'Come on in and have a drink. Cyril will be with us in a moment.' From the bathroom next to the main bedroom the sound of running water had finally stopped.

Rose placed the bottle she had bought alongside others on the work surface. 'My goodness, how many people are you expecting?' Rose asked, wide-eyed, when she saw the amount of food that had been prepared.

'Just a few. Excuse me.' Someone was ringing the doorbell.

At that moment Cyril appeared, freshly shaved and smartly dressed although the ingrained soil would never wash from his hands no matter how hard he scrubbed.

'This is for you.' She handed Cyril the card and present. 'You shouldn't have,' he said as he opened the card. It contained a simple birthday greeting. Rose knew he would not have appreciated a humorous or lewd card. His pleasure was evident as he unwrapped the small watercolour. 'That's real 'ansome,' he said, unsure whether to kiss her. 'We'll hang that in the living-room.'

Rose smiled. He would see more of it if he hung it in his potting shed.

By seven o'clock all of the guests had arrived. There were eleven people in total, which was about as many as the bungalow could comfortably hold. Rose knew only the Clarkes, Jack and Nathan Brown. It was Jack who raised his glass and proposed a toast to Cyril, who blushed and looked embarrassed. 'Here's to the next decade,' he added, smiling at the surprise on Rose's face.

She had had no idea it was his sixtieth birthday; she had imagined him to be the same age as Doreen. His face was lived-in and weatherbeaten but he moved and walked like a much younger man. Perhaps all those years in the mine and now the gardening had kept him fit. She and Jack made conversation with Cyril's friends, most of whom had also been miners. Later, when Rose went outside to get some fresh air and to smoke a cigarette, Doreen joined her. 'I heard about Dave Fox. I didn't like to say anything to Jack, but why are they persecuting him?'

Rose never understood just how Doreen managed to know everything that went on within the area. 'I think it's a case of bad luck, of being in the wrong place at the wrong time.'

'He'd never hurt a fly, that one. And they haven't found who strangled that poor chile yet. It's a disgrace, that's what I call it. I know what I'd do to 'en if I got my hands on 'im.'

'What would you do?'

Neither of them had heard Nathan approach. He looked better than the last time Rose has seen him but it would be a very long time before he adjusted to living alone.

'It wouldn't be ladylike to tell you,' Doreen said. 'Now, you have a chat with Rose while I make sure everyone's got enough to eat and drink.'

Rose, for once lost for words, had no idea how to initiate a conversation with Nathan. Out of desperation she asked 'What do you make of it all?'

Nathan looked at his highly polished shoes. 'Girls shouldn't be out on their own at night. It isn't safe.'

'But it was daylight, at least when the first two were attacked.' She was shocked at his attitude. His views might have been expected from a much older male but Nathan was barely forty. But Doreen had told her of the strong religious views his mother had held. No doubt her influence was strong. 'How are you managing?' she asked, to change the subject and cover her own reaction.

'As well as possible. I've got to find something to do, I've got too much time on my hands now. I didn't realise how much of the day was spent running around after Mother.'

She sensed belated resentment in his tone. Had he realised he had wasted most of his life? Or was the resentment for what his mother had made him?

Jack came out to rescue her. 'You haven't eaten,' he said handing her a plate filled with food. 'And your glass is empty. Nathan, can I get you another beer?'

'Thank you.' He handed Jack his glass and they both followed him back into the kitchen.

'He doesn't have a lot in the way of social graces,' Jack commented when Nathan left, the first to go home.

'I know, but it's hardly surprising given the life he's led. At least he came. Do you think we should make a move?'

'Yes. Let's walk up to the Cornish Arms and order a taxi from there.'

'We're off now, Doreen. Thank you for a lovely evening.' Rose turned to wish Cyril all the best then picked up her handbag.

'Oh, Rose, dear, I forgot. You wouldn't drop this in to Nathan on your way, would you.' Doreen had packed up some of the food which had been left, which was almost as much as had been consumed. 'He can have it for his croust tomorrow.'

'Of course.' They had to pass the house on their way to the pub.

'You know the number?'

'Yes.'

Jack carried the bag and they walked the short distance to what had once been Phyllis Brown's house. Rose lifted the plaited bronze knocker and let it fall. It was more than a minute before Nathan answered the door. He looked puzzled, as if, for a second, he did not recognise them.

'Doreen asked us to come.'

'There's some bits and pieces left over,' Jack added, handing him the bag of food.

'I'll thank her in the morning.' The door was closed before they could say anything else.

Jack raised his eyebrows and smiled at Rose. 'That's the first man I've encountered who hasn't fallen for either your charm or your beauty. I like that painting of the estuary, by the way. It's not one I've seen before.'

'I did it ages ago.'

'What's up?' Jack asked as they made their way to the pub.

'Nothing.' But Rose was thinking Nathan hadn't wasted time since his mother's death. There had been no television in the house when Phyllis was alive, she had considered it to be a corrupting influence although, for some reason, the radio held no such dangers. Rose had seen through the net curtains the flickering of a screen although the volume must have been turned down because the windows were not double-glazed and no sound had been heard from the doorstep even when Nathan opened the door. Odd, though, that ghostly flickering.

They had time for one drink before their taxi arrived. To Jack's surprise Rose gave her address. Normally he would have been dropped off first.

They went into the house together. 'Put the kettle on, Jack, I just want to look at something.'

He did so then went to the sitting-room. 'We're going to watch television?' She was studying the relevant page of the *Western Morning News*.

'No, of course not.' But her question had been answered. There were no black and white films on television that evening. 'I was curious about something.'

'When aren't you? And you know what curiosity did.'

Before she could come out with a suitable retort, Jack kissed her. I hope you're wrong, Jack, she thought as she kissed him back.

CHAPTER TWELVE

Jack had left Rose's house early on Sunday morning. Even though she usually took Sundays off she had hinted, quite strongly, that she didn't want to waste the excellent light. He also sensed something was troubling her, something which he knew she would refuse to discuss with him, because he could read her moods. There had been a slight coolness between them when he left. 'I ought to be used to it by now,' he told himself as he drove to Camborne on Monday morning. He had spent Sunday lunchtime in the pub then gone home for a doze in front of the television regretting his stupidity in wasting the day.

There were two things which puzzled him.

Why did Dave Fox's name keep cropping up and what, if anything, did Rod Hill have to do with things? There was no proof he had had an affair with an under-age girl, only her say-so and that had been retracted. It could, however, still be true. I'll speak to him myself, he decided. Both Fox and Hill were relative newcomers to the area and the crimes had taken place since their arrival.

The officers from Plymouth were still working alongside them on the case but it was only a matter of time before another murder required their presence elsewhere. The attacks seemed to have been planned, each taking place where there were no houses and, in the latter two incidents, where there was no road to allow a witness to pass. Would Fox or Hill have this local knowledge? But whoever was guilty must have followed the girls, they surely couldn't have happened across three females on their own by chance.

He completed a few bits of outstanding paperwork then rang Rod Hill to see if he was at home. A few minutes later Jack was back in his car.

Laura Penfold bitterly regretted her decision to look after a neighbour's dog for the weekend. It was a large, shaggy mongrel which seemed to fill her cottage and which also seemed determined to trip Trevor up every time he moved.

'Can't you do something with that bloody thing?' he'd demanded on Sunday morning when the dog, whose name, for some reason, was Petesy, rested its paws on the kitchen table and tried to take a slice of Cornish hog's pudding from Trevor's breakfast plate. He tapped it on the nose with his knife and continued to eat.

'It's only until tomorrow,' Laura told him. 'It's the first break they've had for ages, and they could hardly miss their son's wedding. He'll be gone by lunchtime then we can do something together.' Trevor was right, she should have refused. Petesy was loveable but had never been disciplined. And he needed walking twice a day. Laura hadn't been able to go out with Trevor the previous evening because she had no idea what Petesy might do in her absence. This had led to one of the numerous arguments which had punctuated their marriage since the days of their honeymoon.

'This is the very last time,' she told Petesy as she fastened his lead on Monday morning. In jeans and a striped top she set off to walk him. Her hair was held high on her head in a towelling band. Trevor, watching from the doorway of their home, could not help smiling at Laura's bouncing corkscrew curls as she tried to keep up with the dog who was pulling at its lead. He knew she would not let it off the lead in case it failed to return when she called. That'll teach her, he thought as he went in to study the sports pages of the Sunday paper, a treat he kept until he could be sure of no interruptions.

Laura reached the Promenade for the third morning in succession. There she encountered other dog walkers who were up and about early. Some had started speaking to her, imagining she was as enamoured of the shaggy dog as they were of their own pets. To avoid them she turned into Morrab Road and then went through the gate to the gardens. Ahead was a figure she recognised. 'Lucy,' she called.

Lucy turned around. Her face was pale but her eyes had lost their dull, lifeless expression. Within seconds Laura had caught her up as she was half-dragged up the slope by Petesy. 'Sit,' she ordered firmly.

Petesy stared at her, tongue lolling and then, surprisingly, did as he was told. 'How are you?'

'Not too bad really. I'm going back to work today. I can't avoid it for ever, and Mum's gone back, too. I just wish they'd find him, Laura. I'm looking over my shoulder all the time.'

'I know. I'm sure there're doing all they can.' They began to walk side by side. 'I just wish I could have given the police more help.'

'Don't think about it now.'

'I went out with some friends on Friday.'

'Did you?' Lucy had sounded proud, as if she had achieved something special. Laura realised that she probably had.

'Yes. I didn't stay late but it was a start. And I've made it up with Sam. I don't know why I was such a bitch to her. I'm seeing her tonight.'

'That's good news.' They had reached the gate at the top of the park. Lucy would continue on towards the hairdresser's where she worked while Laura would turn back and retrace her route. 'And I saw Jason. Well, not to speak to. He was with another girl so that's obviously over. She's someone down on holiday so that won't last either. She's called Liz, apparently. I know all this because one of my friends went over to speak to him.' She smiled wanly. 'She has to know everything that's going on.'

'You don't sound too upset about it.'

'I'm not. It's for the best really. And Sam was pleased.'

Laura nodded, not quite sure why that might be. Maybe Sam had been jealous of the relationship. Anyway, she would relay the good news to Rose as soon as she got rid of the dog. 'Take care, Lucy,' she said, realising too late how her words must sound after what had happened to her. 'Look, why don't you and your mum come over tomorrow evening. Trevor's sailing, we can have a drink and some supper.'

'Thanks. I'll check with Mum and let you know.'

Laura began the walk home. Her neighbours had said they would be back by twelve. If Trevor took himself off to the pub she would ring Rose for a gossip and join him later.

Rose's face was browner than ever. All of Sunday and most of Monday had been out spent of doors. As soon as Jack had left she had thrown on her painting clothes and set off in the car. Already an idea had formed in her mind for her next piece of work.

She had parked in a lay-by on the Lizard Peninsular and clambered down to the shoreline. There, facing Poldhu Point, she had set up her easel. There was no one in sight, she had had the place to herself. To her right was the glistening sea with a few small breakers near the shore. Ahead was a cliff, rising steeply and covered with wind-toughened grass at the top and, at her feet and spreading into the distance, were smooth boulders, their surfaces treacherous with hanks of bladder wrack and bright green slime which Rose thought might be called dulce. In the rock-pools the tendrils of anemones floated and shrimp-like creatures darted for cover. This she would capture in oils, the colours predominantly greens.

By Monday afternoon she had made a good start and returned home satisfied. The work would need to be completed quickly because the tide altered by roughly an hour each day and soon the water would cover the boulders during the hours when the light was right.

She showered away the heat and grains of sand and wrapped herself in her towelling robe. Feeling virtuous she went down to open some wine. 'I should've known,' she said no more than five minutes later when Laura appeared, her face also flushed from the sun.

'Known what?'

'That I couldn't have an hour to myself.'

'What on earth are you talking about? You've been out all day, I've kept trying to ring you.' Without asking, Laura took a glass from the cupboard and held it out to Rose with a fake girlish smile.

Rose laughed. 'Go on, help yourself. I thought Trevor was home.'

'He is. He's gone fishing.'

Rose nodded. She knew that Laura meant with rod and line and bait in the bay. A strange hobby for a deep sea fisherman but Trevor was not the only one who enjoyed it. 'So you're bored and decided to come and annoy me.'

Laura grinned. 'Yes, that's about right. Oh, I saw Lucy this morning, she's gone back to work.'

'Good. It'll help take her mind off it all.'

'I suppose so. And her boyfriend's now out of the picture.'

'What? Because of what happened?' Rose was indignant on Lucy's behalf.

'Not exactly. I got the impression that it was more Lucy's decision than his. Gwen told me she hadn't been returning his calls. Anyway, she saw him with someone else and she says that's fine by her.'

'He didn't waste time.' Rose sipped her wine and reached for her cigarettes.

'I don't suppose he's got much time. The girl's down here on holiday.'

'How on earth do you know that?'

'You're not the only one with too much

curiosity. Lucy's friend spoke to Jason and Lucy related the gist of the conversation to me.'

Down on holiday. Another teenage girl. 'Where does she live?'

Laura laughed. 'You've got me there. I didn't get as far as finding that out, only that her name's Liz. Why?'

'I just wondered.'

'Come on, Rose, I can see by your face there's more to it than that.'

'All right, there is. And I'm going to have to tell Jack.' She paused. If her suspicions were correct then Lucy Chandler might be in trouble. 'Dave Fox was taken in for questioning again.'

'Rose, you've lost me already.'

'Dave, my gardener. He was working on someone's garden at a time when no one was home and the place got broken into. Fortunately the police now seem satisfied that it happened some time after he left.'

'Rose, what have you got yourself into now?' Laura was frowning as she pushed her glass around the table. Her friend's aptitude to land in trouble worried her.

Over a second glass of wine Rose explained her theory.

'If that's true, and I think you might be right

after what you told me before about Jason, there's unhappiness in store for several people. And, yes, you do have to tell Jack. But can any of this be connected to what's happened to those girls?'

Rose shook her head. 'Impossible to guess. But there are just too many connections for it to be coincidence.'

'Look, I'm going now. Trevor promised he wouldn't be late, which is no guarantee he won't be, but I'd rather be there when he gets back.' Laura stood and picked up her keys which lay on the table. 'Ring Jack the minute I've gone.'

'I will.' Rose watched from the doorway until Laura was out of sight then went straight to the telephone. I should've mentioned this on Saturday, she thought, or even on Sunday morning. If I'd done so then I might have prevented this robbery and the anguish Dave and Eva have been through.

'Yes?'

'It's me, Rose.' She was surprised at the abruptness of Jack's tone when he answered his telephone.

'It's been a long day.'

'Well, I won't keep you. It's just that, well, there's something I think you ought to know. It's all guesswork, really, and it mightn't be the same girl . . .'

'For God's sake, Rose, what are you talking about?'

'There's no need to snap.' She waited.

'All right, I apologise. Start from the beginning.'

'Lucy Chandler's ex-boyfriend, Jason Evans, is seeing a girl called Liz. I don't know her surname or her address, only the fact that she's down here on holiday. I also happen to know that the granddaughter of the family who were burgled is called Liz and that she's staying with them.'

'So?'

'Come on, Jack, think about it. Perhaps she told Jason that no one would be in that day.'

'So Jason's our thief. Just like that you've solved several cases on the assumption of a girl's first name.'

I don't know why I bother, she thought as she inhaled deeply. 'On a bit more than that, actually. Jason is unemployed yet he gave Lucy a very expensive looking watch.'

'Perhaps he's got savings, perhaps his parents give him hand outs.'

'Okay, Jack. Goodbye. I'll speak to you another time.' She hung up. Of course Jack was right, she had next to nothing to go on but it did all seem to fit. He could at least have listened politely instead of biting her head off. And then she felt guilty. He's tired, probably very tired and these burglaries are nothing in comparison to rape and murder. Her hand was on the receiver to ring him back when her own phone rang.

'I'll send someone round to speak to Jason Evans. I'm sorry, Rose, I'm tired and hungry and the lack of progress in the Nicky Rolland case is getting to us all. I shouldn't have taken it out on you. I thought when we had Dave Fox in again we might be getting somewhere and I've also had another word with Rod Hill. Witnesses prove he was in the pub all of that Sunday evening and he was seen in his garden around the time of Helen Trehearne was attacked. It looks as if he's in the clear.' He sighed. 'Rose Trevelyan, you're a very trying woman but I love you.'

Rose's grip on the receiver tightened. It was rarely that Jack voiced his emotions and it always took her by surprise. Do I love him, she wondered. Yes, I do, in a way. In lots of ways. She had known that for some time but to admit it would lead Jack to expect more than she could offer him.

'Friends?' he asked, half guessing at what was going through her mind.

‘Yes, friends. Will you let me know the outcome?’

‘If I can. I’ll be in touch. And, thanks, Rose.’

She, too, was tired and hungry, but nicely tired, from a surfeit of sunshine and fresh air and satisfying work. It was time to make something to eat.

Later, she was thinking there was something almost decadent about going to bed early, when the sun was still shining, and lying in bed with the curtains undrawn, reading until darkness made it impossible to continue. But this is what she did. And then she closed her eyes and tried to decide what to do about the one thing she had not mentioned to Jack.

CHAPTER THIRTEEN

Doreen called in to see Nathan briefly on her way to work. She was sure she had persuaded him to start looking for a job and she wanted to keep the pressure up. The only way to succeed with him was to keep nagging until he gave in. As she crossed the road she was aware of the heat which was already building up and knew that she would be exhausted by the time she had finished both of her cleaning jobs that day.

It was not quite eight o'clock but Nathan was dressed, his face smooth from recent shaving. It pleased her to see him continuing to take care of himself. Many men didn't bother when they were left on their own. She doubted that Cyril would bother to come into the house except to sleep if anything happened to her.

'I've made a few calls,' Nathan told her. 'One sounds quite hopeful. I've got to go and see old man Trevean soon. The trouble is the car's been playing me up and it's got to go into the garage. They're more trouble than they're worth at times.'

'I'm real gladdened, Nathan. If you need a lift, come over and tell me. Otherwise don't forget to let me know how you get on.' Satisfied that all was well and her tactics had worked Doreen got into her car and drove off to her first cleaning job of the day.

Later that evening, having washed up their supper dishes and tidied the kitchen she made two pint mugs of tea. One she took out to Cyril who was in a world of his own, busy with the watering-can, a cloud of pipe smoke encircling his head. The second she placed by the telephone. She was in the mood for a chat and decided to ring a couple of friends. It was Rose's number she dialled first. 'How's Evelyn getting along?'

'Dad says she's tired a lot of the time but she's making slow progress.' There wasn't much more she could say to the numerous but well meaning enquiries.

'That's the main thing. Sounds a bit like Nathan really. He's keeping that house like a new pin, much to my amazement. And now, God bless 'en, he's got hisself a television and video. I'm surprised he knows how the thing do work. And to cap it all, this morning he tells me he's got an interview for a job. Good luck to 'im, that's what I say.'

Rose smiled as Doreen paused for breath and took a noisy sip of her tea, one of the many mugfuls she drank in the course of a day. But why shouldn't Nathan make progress? Look at Barry, a man Rose had believed to have been too old, too set in his ways to ever change. Now he was buying new clothes and decorating his flat. Nathan was proving to be stronger than he had appeared to most people but Rose has sensed some inner strength. As with the fête, Doreen was not afraid to show how proud of him she was.

She listened to Doreen's chatter for a couple more minutes then tactfully ended the conversation by saying she was in the middle of cooking her meal and didn't want it to spoil. Farm work, Doreen had said, it was work Nathan was used to and he would be ideally suited to it because he wouldn't have to make small talk or try to please people from behind a counter or a desk. Things were looking good for him.

Remaining beside the telephone it occurred to Rose that she had not yet spoken to her mother since her return home from hospital. 'She's resting,' her father had told her when she called on Saturday evening, and again when she rang on Sunday. 'They told us to expect that she'd be very tired for a while.'

'Don't disturb her, just tell her I rang and give her my love.' She wanted very much to hear Evelyn's voice, to be reassured that she really was making progress, but to wake her might delay that progress.

'She had an hour or so sitting in the garden,' Arthur told his daughter when he phoned her on Tuesday. 'I've made her go up for a lie down, she looks a bit grey. You know your mother, Rose, she's as stubborn as you. She insists she's fine when it's obvious she isn't.'

'I'll come up, Dad. You need a break and I can make sure she does as she's told.'

Arthur snorted. 'Fat chance of that after all these years. But no, maybe next week. I'd, well, it sounds daft as we've never been apart, but I'd like her to myself at the moment. It's a chance to repay the way she's always looked after me.'

Rose felt tears in her eyes. Even as a child she had known her parents' marriage was somehow different from others. They had worked side by side on the farm, never far apart and had continued in that way since their retirement. She often wondered whether it was because she had been led by example or whether it was pure luck that she had picked the man who had made her so happy. He picked me, really, Rose thought, recalling how insistent David had been, how, after only a fortnight he had told her he loved her. They had married within a year. We were so young, we could have been so wrong, she thought. 'All right, but remember you can ring me at any time and I'll come.'

It had been another hot day with a visit to the library followed by the final session on the Poldhu painting. 'I'm improving,' Rose told herself as she stood scrutinising the canvas which was propped against the larder wall. But she felt restless, her father's call had disturbed her. She prayed he wasn't holding anything back, that her mother was simply tired, no more than that. She picked up her bag, locked the kitchen door behind her and, having made sure her mobile phone was charged up and on, walked quickly down the hill. She had decided upon a circular route, a long walk to ensure she would sleep. Having crossed Newlyn Green she walked up Alexandra Road, turned right into Alverton Road and continued on up the steep hill which was Penalverne Drive. Keeeping up the pace, her calf muscles began to ache.

She could feel the steady beating of her heart and took slower, longer breaths until she finally came to West Cornwall Hospital. She waited to cross the road wondering whether her choice of direction had some Freudian connection. There was no reason to have come this way, there was far more to see along the Promenade.

The homeward journey was downhill. She reached the top of Causewayhead and kept walking towards the sea. There was a queue for the cinema but she couldn't decide which of the three films was attracting such a crowd. None of them appealed to her. By the time she was back in Newlyn she was totally calm and in need of a rest. I'll repay Laura with an unexpected visit, she decided as she neared her house. When Laura let her in Rose regretted her impulse because her friend already had company. Gwen and Lucy Chandler were seated in her living-room, gin and tonics in their hands.

'Don't be stupid, the more the merrier,' Laura

said when Rose apologised and said she'd leave. 'We're celebrating their return to work. I take it you won't say no to a stiff gin even if you are dressed like a tramp.' She winked at Rose. Rose looked down. Her rope espadrilles had seen better days, her denim skirt was splattered with paint, only her blouse was tidy. She probably had paint in her hair, too, because she had left it loose that day. Clothes had never meant much to her unless she was going somewhere special.

Gwen and Lucy both appeared more relaxed than when she had last seen them but there was a long way to go yet. Rose had come for a gossip with Laura but knew it would not be appropriate. She allowed the other women to run the conversation.

'It wasn't easy on Monday,' Lucy said. 'I know people had guessed but they didn't say anything.' She shook her head. 'I'm sorry, I must stop talking about it.'

'We're making some changes,' Gwen continued. 'Something like this brings home to you that life is for living. When I think of that other poor girl.' Her hand shook as she reached for her drink. 'Anyway, we've decided to redecorate Lucy's bedroom as a start. She's picked the paper and I'm going to make the curtains. I used to sew a lot when the children were small. Unfortunately I lent my sewing-machine to my daughter-in-law and I've never seen it since.'

'Borrow mine,' Rose said. 'It hasn't been out of the cupboard for years. I used to make my own clothes in the days when it was cheaper than buying them.'

'Could I?'

'If you're going to be here for a while I'll go home and bring it down in the car then give you both a lift home.'

'I'd really appreciate that.' Gwen smiled. It was the first time Rose had seen her do so.

'Shall I come and give you a hand?' Lucy asked.

Rose was surprised at the offer but agreed. They began the climb up the hill. Rose regretted having sat down as her legs were now protesting at more effort but she would soak in the bath later.

'I heard you're no longer with Jason,' Rose said to break the silence as they passed the Red Lion. The harbour, to their left, glinted in the evening sunshine.

Lucy nodded but didn't speak because just then a car stopped on the opposite side of the road.

'Lovely evening,' Doreen Clarke said as she stuck her head out of the driver's window.

Rose was about to respond when she noticed the passenger. The expression of panic on his face was so fleeting that she wasn't sure it had been there at all.

'I've just taken Nathan up to Harry Trevean's place. Looks like he'll be starting work there. Nathan's car's been playing up so it's in the garage and as it's such good weather we came back the long way so's we could admire the view.' Doreen was staring pointedly at Lucy, waiting for an introduction.

'This is Lucy Chandler,' she said. 'Lucy, this is my friend, Doreen Clarke and Nathan Brown.'

Lucy said a polite hello but there was no chance for further conversation because two cars were behind Doreen's waiting for her to drive on. One of the drivers tooted his horn. Doreen put the car into gear, gave a quick wave and disappeared down the hill.

'I'll just get a cloth,' Rose said when they were in the larder. The sewing-machine held a layer of dust. It was many years old but a good one, made from wood and steel in the days before plastic was popular. Together they carried it to the back seat of Rose's car then drove back the way they had walked.

Gwen was ready to leave when they arrived so they went straight off.

'I'm really grateful,' Gwen told her as she and Lucy got the machine out of the car. 'I'll look after it and bring it back the minute I've finished.'

'There's no rush. As I said, I haven't used it in years.'

Rose went home and ran a bath. She sank beneath the water and lay there for some time. 'There's only one way to find out,' she said aloud. 'If you don't know, ask.'

Eva's smile was infectious. 'Good news?' Dave asked when he came home from work.

'I've got a job.'

He put the kettle on while she explained how she had managed to talk the landlord of a Penzance pub into giving her a trial. 'One of the staff left unexpectedly and I happened to walk in at the right time. Perhaps our luck is changing. Well, I said I'd do anything, serving behind the bar, waitressing, whatever they wanted. They do lunches and dinners and it's always busy apparently. The only thing is I'll have to do some evening shifts.'

Dave reached for her and stroked her hair. It seemed as animated as she was. 'That's fine by me. You must live the way you want to. Now, are you coming with me this evening?'

'Yes.' She didn't know how he did it; all day his work was physical and he could still spend the evenings renovating the barn. It was gradually taking shape but even to Eva it was obvious there were many more months of hard work before it was habitable and a lot more work after that. But she would help him. Under his directions she was sure there were things of which she would be capable. All that marred the future was the fact that a murderer was out there somewhere and that she and the police had believed it possible that Dave might have committed it. That, and the question of the robbery at the Johnson's bungalow.

Barry Rowe came backwards down the stepladder, a paint tray and roller in one hand. He stood back with satisfaction and admired his achievement through his glasses which were spotted with paint. Already the flat looked brighter and cleaner. He had decided upon plain walls as the rooms were small, and light, cheerful colours ranging through white gloss to primrose and pale peach emulsion. Daphne Hill had been kind enough to bring him some colour charts which she'd picked up during one of her lunch breaks. Already he could picture the new furniture; pale pine or some other light wood and patterned curtains which incorporated the colours of the rooms. And new bed linen.

The shop bell rang. Barry cursed. He had forgotten to tell the company that there was a back entrance to the flat. Downstairs waited the man who had come to sell him a new kitchen. Barry had hoped to have Rose there to give him advice but he had been assured that the representative would offer a plan to make the most of whatever space was available.

Barry laughed. I'm actually enjoying this, he thought as he went to let the man in.

Only later, when he had paid a hefty deposit and cleaned his paintbrushes did he give Daphne and Rod another thought. She had told him that an Inspector Pearce had been out to see Rod. If Jack's involved, Barry thought, then it's serious. He liked Daphne and didn't want to lose her but he feared he would if things turned out badly for Rod Hill.

He realised it was late, light was fading from the sky, and that he was hungry. It would be nice to eat out, to not bother to cook something, but it was not a pleasure he enjoyed alone and it was too late to ring Rose or anyone else.

He opened the kitchen window and flapped his hands at the low roof opposite, to no effect. The pair of herring-gulls continued to squawk raucously. At least the noise was not as unbearable as earlier in the year when they were mating. He had had some razor wire placed around his defunct chimney-pot to stop gulls nesting there and wished his neighbours would do the same.

He cooked scrambled eggs, sausages and beans and sat down to eat hoping that Rose would be free to go to Plymouth with him on Sunday and help him choose the furniture. The old stuff would go to some charity or other.

The telephone rang just as he picked up his knife and fork. He had been thinking of Rose, it had to be her.

'Hello, Barry, it's Daphne. Look, I just thought I'd let you know the police have been around here asking questions and they seem satisfied that Rod's in the clear. I know it could've waited until the morning but I'm so pleased. Rod is, too, of course, but he's a bit down because he's still afraid people'll find out about the past. Anyway, we're having a bit of a do on Saturday night. We've decided not to bury our heads in the sand any longer. If people do find out, then so be it.

It's up to them to decide how they feel, not us. So will you come?'

'I'd love to. Thank you.'

Daphne laughed. 'Good. It's daft, really, but we've invited neighbours we've hardly spoken to. We'll know you better than we know anyone else.'

'It'll give me a chance to widen my circle of acquaintances, too.' It had taken him many years but he was beginning to realise just how limited his life was. When he first met Rose he had hoped for different things. Yes, he still loved her, he always would, but he had to accept that the time for hoping was long gone. I shall certainly go, he decided as he sat down to his cooling food, and I shall go alone. He would order a taxi to take him there and ring for another when it was time to leave.

Jack Pearce looked at his face in the mirror in the bathroom and hoped that it was the light rather than the way he felt which gave his skin that greyish tinge.

I ought to phone her, he thought as he splashed cold water into his eyes. I ought to let her know she was right. But how will she feel when she realises we've had to speak to Samantha Jago and Lucy Chandler; Lucy, who had already been through enough.

Jack pushed open the French doors which led to his secluded garden. The people upstairs were rarely at home and they could only overlook him if they happened to be standing in the window. As he had no inclination to sunbathe nude, or to sunbathe at all, it hardly mattered.

The air was full of the scent of lavender in which numerous bees flitted from stem to stem. The garden had been established long before he moved in and he had made no attempt to alter it. The summer flowering shrubs were now coming into their own and filled the narrow borders with colour.

He strolled around the perimeter, a glass of beer untouched in his hand. Jason Evans had been interviewed and charged even though his parents had miraculously appeared from somewhere bringing with them a solicitor.

I will tell her, he decided, it's only fair. But deep down he was aware it was also an excuse to speak to her. She took a long time to answer.

'Hello?' Rose was as terse as he had been when she rang him.

'Am I disturbing you?'

'Yes. I was in the bath.' She did not add that

the water was cold and she'd been about to get out.

'We've charged Jason Evans,' he told her without preamble hoping the news would make her more amiable.

'Good heavens.'

'You were right. He and one of his mates have been breaking and entering to make ends meet. They only took small, easily saleable objects, things they could carry without the need of transport. Neither of them has any previous form and it was pure luck they weren't caught sooner.

'You were right about the girl, Liz. Only she knew nothing about it. She was horrified. She'd innocently told Jason their plans for the day, although she didn't know that Dave Fox would be on the scene in the morning and therefore assumed he was responsible.

'The thing is, Rose, to give the boy his due, he refuses to implicate Lucy. The night she was raped he broke into a place nearby He claims they'd argued and she went off in a mood and it was only then he decided to do the job. My feeling is that he wanted to use her as his look-out and she refused and that's why they argued.'

'What'll happen to her?' She could probably

be charged as an accessory if she had known what Jason was up to and failed to report it.

'I don't know.'

'Jack, can you just do nothing? I mean, surely she's learnt her lesson after what happened to her that evening.'

Jack thought about it. There were some who would say it was poetic justice, if carried a little too far; the criminal becomes the victim of crime. But he was a police officer, if he turned a blind eye to one thing where would it lead in the end? 'No, Rose, I can't just do nothing. We'll speak to her once more. If she denies it then we'll accept what she says. You'll just have to trust me.

'Anyway, how's Evelyn?'

'I'm not sure, really. Dad says she's very tired and each time I've rung she's been resting. I'm going up next week to see for myself.'

'If there's anything I can do, such as drive you, you know where I am.'

'Thanks, Jack. And thank you for letting me know about Jason.'

'Are you sure you wouldn't like a job with the Devon and Cornwall police? We might never have got Evans without the information you gave us.'

'Information?' Rose was indignant. 'I bloody

well solved the case for you.' During one of their telephone calls she had finally mentioned the expensive watch Lucy had said Jason had given her. As Rose had suspected, it turned out to be stolen.

'Then I owe you a meal. Fancy a night out soon? Before you go away?'

'I never say no to free food and drink.'

'How about the Seafarer's on Saturday night?'

'Wonderful. You're on.'

'I'll ring you to confirm a time.'

He didn't mention Nichola Rolland, Rose thought after she'd hung up. And there was something I didn't mention either, she realised as she pulled the damp towel closer to her body and went back up to the bathroom to rub almond scented moisturiser into her skin.

CHAPTER FOURTEEN

The Wednesday classes seemed to come around so quickly. Rose had decided that they would concentrate on charcoal tonight. She hoped to convey that in this medium fewer lines were more effective, and she had some excellent examples to illustrate that simplicity was the key to a good piece of work.

Without realising it she had sketched the head and shoulders of Nathan Brown on her notebook. Sticking the pencil behind her ear she decided she needed to talk to Doreen about him before she spoke to Jack. She knew now what it was about that library book that had disturbed her. I'll pop over tomorrow evening,' she said, talking aloud as she often did when on her own. It would make no difference to Cyril who would be out watering the plants or searching for invisible weeds.

It was a dullish sort of day with a stiff breeze. The washing flapped on the line, the sheets as white as the clouds which were beginning to mass and cover the bay. She watered her own plants as there was no direct sun nor any sign of rain, then did some shopping in Newlyn. For some reason she was not in the mood to paint.

The weekend looks like being as busy as the week has been, she thought as she unlocked the gallery door. There was dinner with Jack on Saturday night to look forward to and a day at the furniture superstores on the outskirts of Plymouth with Barry on Sunday to follow. He had rung to finalise the arrangement. And soon I'll see Mum again. Her father had agreed that Monday would be a suitable day to arrive. 'She'll have had just over a week to recover by then and she's really looking forward to seeing you. I'll put her on.'

On the two occasions upon which Rose had now spoken to Evelyn she had noticed how much weaker her voice had sounded.

'I wish you'd all stop fussing,' Evelyn had said pretending annoyance but touched by their concern. Rose had passed on her friends' messages. Now she wanted to judge for herself how well her mother really was.

'Hi.'

Rose turned around. Joyce Jago stood behind her. She was smiling. 'I'm glad I caught you early. I just wanted to tell you that Sam seems back to her old self now. She and Lucy have made it up, and I heard that the boy that caused the trouble between them has been arrested.'

'Yes, I heard that, too.'

'Did you?' Joyce seemed surprised until she remembered that Rose was supposed to be seeing a detective inspector. 'Anyway, a very nice female officer came to have a word with Sam. I thought that would bring the house down and set her off again but no, she sat down and told me all about it afterwards.'

Sam had lied for Lucy but even if she had suspected there was more to it than meeting Jason, Rose doubted she knew about his short-lived criminal career.

'Anyway, that seems to be the end of it.'

'Good. Can you give me a hand with the chairs?'

Thank you Jack, she thought later as she tried, mostly unsuccessfully, to get her point across to the class.

She walked home slowly, glancing now and then at the sky but it held no clues as to the following day's weather. In West Cornwall it was a case of waking up and looking out of the window to see what the day would bring. There was a swell on the sea and the tang of salt and seaweed in the air. Rose breathed deeply, clearing her lungs after the stuffy gallery annexe. It was one of those old, high-ceilinged buildings which was draughty and cold in the winter and equally as uncomfortable in the summer. Only the gallery itself had been modernised, the paintings hung amidst glass and chrome.

The shrill voices of the few remaining children in the playground carried through the air, as did the sound of gulls perched on the railings hoping for scraps of food from people sitting in the shelters. Rose leant on the railings, her canvas bag at her feet. The tide was ebbing, running back over the row of flat boulders that edged the banks of pebbles. Few waders would come to feed now, they had migrated for the summer. An occasional turnstone might be seen, even a ringed plover, hardly discernable amongst the stones but there was no chance of that tonight as there were people on the beach and a dog barking madly as it chased the gulls. On the horizon the sea was the colour of bruising before it began to fade; nearer the shore it was lighter, bluer but the whole was capped with white horses. The wind whipped through her linen jacket and tugged at her hair, carrying with it a strong smell of brine. A trawler was coming home, its beams still spread. Not Trevor, he had only sailed the day before, but someone's husband or son returning safely. This time. Nichola Rolland had not returned home safely and Lucy Chandler had escaped with her life. Which reminded Rose of her intention to speak to Doreen Clarke in the morning.

Nathan Brown did not feel like watching the video again. Perhaps it was because he had finally found employment, outdoor work which he enjoyed, had always enjoyed until his mother's illness had taken it away from him, just as she, when fit, had taken every other pleasure away from him. He was starting to realise just how much he had disliked her.

I know I'm not an educated man, he thought as he pottered around outside the house dead-heading the ugly hydrangeas which had flowered earlier than usual. His mother had liked them and seemed unconcerned that in the winter there was nothing to see other than their dead-looking spiky twigs. Tomorrow he would cut the sloping lawn. It gave him backache but needed to be done; in the evening if the day was hot. Soon he would be fit again, fit but not worn out as he had been when he was running constant errands for his mother. Soon he would spend his days on the farm come rain or shine and his hands would be encrusted with dirt and he wouldn't have to listen to that sharp voice admonishing him not to come to the table until his nails were clean. As if they ever could be when you worked on a farm.

He went through the house carrying the desiccated flower heads and threw them in the bin outside the back door. The house had not been redecorated for as long as he could remember but he had no intention of doing anything about it. What he did intend doing was to sell it, just as it was. Whoever bought it would have their own ideas about paper and paint, and then he would buy somewhere smaller, somewhere without a back-breaking slope of a garden, somewhere where he could grow pretty things and take a woman home without the ghost of his mother watching.

Knowing he must eat but not feeling hungry, he went back to the dismal kitchen and took out a loaf of bread. Something warm hit his hand as he drew the serrated knife through the crust. It was a teardrop. Nathan was shocked to find he was crying. He knew that no woman would want him because he had no idea at all how to talk to them. He stuffed his knuckles in his mouth to stop the sound of his sobbing from echoing around his drab surroundings.

Rose was at Nancherrow Valley. She had driven to St Just then on to Cape Cornwall searching for somewhere suitable to work. She was making a brief return to landscapes in watercolours, mainly to keep her hand in. Here the scenery was far different from the soft, sandy beaches and picturesque streets of St Ives, only a few miles distant. Here was true ruggedness: piles of ancient stones balanced precariously, nothing but sloping scrubland, no trees, no birdsong, and all around the remains of tin mines which had fallen into decay. Even on a warm summer day it was bleak, almost eerie. Rose had finally found a scene which would work. She got out of the car and locked it and walked a little way into the valley. To her right were craggy cliffs, to her left a steep slope covered now with verdant growth, as was the single stack of a disused mine. The low ruins of brickwork were vaguely discernable beneath layers of growth of a weed she could not identify. Between the two slopes a triangle of sea was visible, glittering beneath a haze. Water and sky blended at the horizon. The view provided a perfect composition. She laid out her ground-sheet, got out her gear and her flask and set to work, being careful to use smaller strokes and a more gentle approach than was necessary with oils.

It was after six by the time she reached Doreen's bungalow. The time had passed quickly. Although she had worn her battered hat Rose hoped she hadn't overdone the sun. Her nose, forearms and shins tingled with the heat.

'You'm all red, maid,' Doreen said when she saw Rose standing outside the kitchen door. 'Come in and have a cold drink.'

Rose smiled. Concern was Doreen's first reaction. She never turned anyone away who just happened to arrive unexpectedly. Doreen opened the fridge and got out some fresh orange juice. 'Is this all right?'

'Fine.'

Above a cotton print dress, tightly belted between generous bosom and ample stomach, Doreen's face was pale, but she worked so hard she rarely saw the sun. 'It's darts tonight so you won't see Cyril 'less you stay late. "I won't be long," 'ee says to me every Thursday but he never gets in until closing time. You can tell when he's lost, he never says a word, it's worse in the winter when they play in the league, you'd think the end of the world had come. Anyway, what brings you over this way?'

'I was almost passing. I was out at Nacherrow and came back via St Ives. I saw this in Penzance the other day and thought you might like it.' Rose handed her a small plastic bag.

'Oh, it's 'ansome, Rose. Thank you so much.' Doreen held up the flimsy scarf with tiny pearls embroidered around the hems. 'There was no need for it, I'm always glad to see you.'

Rose knew that but she and Cyril kept her supplied with fruit and vegetables, flowers and cakes. She had nothing to offer in return except the occasional small gift or some tobacco for Cyril.

'Now you've drunk the orange, how about a glass of stout? I always have a couple on Cyril's night out. It's only fair, that's what I say.'

'Just the one, Doreen, I've got the car.' Rose knew that the gift had embarrassed her even though it also gave her pleasure.

'How's Nathan?'

'He's doing fine. Better than I expected.' She flipped the top off two bottles of dark beer and handed Rose a thick ridged glass. 'He's starting work next Monday, which'll do 'im good. No man should be without a job. And he's talking of selling up. I think the solicitor put that idea in his head. Nathan doesn't get too many of his own. Besides, that place is so gloomy.'

'Doreen, do you remember the other night when I saw you both in Newlyn?'

'Course I do. I'm not senile.'

'Well, did Nathan say anything?'

'He said quite a bit.'

'About Lucy Chandler, I mean. Do you think he knows her?'

'I doubt it. Why?'

Rose shrugged and brushed back a few tendrils which had strayed from the clip which held her hair at the nape of her neck. 'The way he looked at her I thought he recognised her.'

'Well he never said anything to me if he did. You can have a cigarette if you like. After Cyril's pipe anything's acceptable.'

Rose reached into her bag and lit up. Doreen fetched a tin ashtray which had the name of a lager written around its rim. 'Who was the maid? Lucy Chandler, you said. I don't know the name.'

'She's the daughter of someone I know.' Rose left it at that.

'Just like poor Nichola Rolland. I can't understand why finding the man that did that to her is taking so long.'

Rose took a long swallow of her drink, enjoying its bitterness. Doreen didn't expect a response to her statement.

'All I can say is that they don't seem to know what they're about at the moment. I mean, fancy arresting Dave Fox of all people. I saw young Eva the other day and she told me about it. At least that's in the past. Oh, and she's got herself a job, too. I'm pleased for 'un. It means she'll have no cause to leave and you can see that Dave dotes on 'er.'

'I think she does on him.'

'You're probably right. Now, have you had your supper yet or would you like a bite with me? Cyril'll buy 'isself a pasty down the pub.'

'No, I'm fine thanks, Doreen. I'd better be off.' She drained her glass and stood, stretching for a second as she felt the stiffness of having sat working for so long.

She was about to unlock the car when she turned to her left to see where the sound of a lawn-mower was coming from. Nathan Brown stood high up in his garden cutting the lawn. It would be rude not to say hello. Rose crossed the road and walked towards him; the air was scented with freshly cut grass.

Nathan looked up and shielded his eyes from the sun which was lower in the sky than when he had begun. 'Mrs Trevelyan,' he said gruffly.

'How are you, Nathan? Doreen told me you'd got a job. I'm very pleased for you.'

He nodded and fiddled with the handle of the mower.

'And she also said you might be moving.'

'I might.' His tone implied it was none of her business. She took a chance and asked directly, 'I wondered if you knew the girl who was with me the other night. Lucy Chandler.'

'The name means nothing to me.'

He's lying, Rose thought, even though Doreen had once told her she believed him to be incapable of an untruth. Unless, she decided, unless I'm right and he doesn't know her name. It had never appeared in the press. 'Are you sure?' Even as she spoke she could hear Jack's voice telling her to leave things alone.

'Look, I'm not standing out here for all the world to hear our conversation. I think you'd better come inside, Mrs Trevelyan.'

She was startled, the invitation was totally unexpected. She went up the steep steps and followed him into the house. After the brightness of the sun it was difficult to focus immediately and when she did she saw what a gloomy place it was. The lower part of the hall walls consisted of brown painted panels which had probably been there since the house was built. Above it was maroon flocked paper. It would not take much imagination to believe the lights were fuelled by gas.

Nathan flung open the door to his right. Here, too, all was brown; the velveteen suite, the curtains and the carpet which was relieved by bold gold swirls. There was an empty fireplace with traces of soot and some heavy furniture. The only modern thing was a television set with a video recorder shelved below it.

Nathan turned to face her. He might be short and squat but he was menacing. His checked shirt was open at the neck revealing a patch of springy black hair flecked with grey. There was loose grass on his shoes and the bottoms of his cord trousers. 'What's going on?'

'Nothing. I was at Doreen's and I came over to see how you were coping.'

'Then why are you asking me about that girl?'

'Because you seemed to recognise her. I meant no harm.' But she didn't recognise you, Rose thought, and you are definitely hiding something. And I'm frightened. Nathan had kicked the front door closed behind them.

'I don't know anything about her, nor about any other girls.'

Girls. Can I be right? Her face must have shown what she was thinking because he took a step towards her.

'Just shut up and mind your own business, why don't you?' His face was red. 'Bloody women. Don't you think I've had enough of them? Why can't you leave me alone?'

Rose took a step backwards. As she bumped into the edge of something her mobile phone rang. She reached into the open top of her shoulder-bag just as Nathan reached for her. Her hand made contact with the phone. If he touched her she would hit him with it. He grabbed the neck of her T-shirt and pushed his face into hers. She could smell onions on his breath.

He snatched the phone from her hand and threw it across the room. It seemed to move in slow motion. Rose watched it hit the wall and fall to the ground, apparently unbroken because it continued to ring. 'Please . . .' she whispered.

But Nathan was pulling her down onto the settee against which she had come to rest. Dear God, he's going to rape me, she thought as his large, calloused hand came down over her nose and mouth. It was then that she saw the fading teeth-marks at the base of his thumb.

No, please don't let it be true. Laura knew her tears must wait. 'I don't know. Have you tried Jack or Barry? Look, you ring Barry, I'll ring Jack. And anyone else I can think of. I'll get straight back to you.'

Shaking, Laura disconnected the line. Jack answered on the second ring. 'Where's Rose?'

'Laura? That's hardly a way to greet an old friend.'

'For God's sake, Jack, where is she?'

Jack stiffened. Please, please, please don't let her be in trouble he prayed. 'I don't know. Why?' He listened and felt the blood drain from his face. 'We'll find her. Who else have you rung?' Together they listed anyone they could think of who knew Rose. 'Ring me back right away, or I'll ring you,' he said, realising too late that if they were trying each other they'd get the engaged signal.

It was Laura who discovered that Rose had been to see Doreen. 'She left about fifteen minutes ago,' Doreen told her. 'Wait a minute. Her car's still outside. I . . .'

'Got to go, Doreen.'

'I'm on my way,' Jack said as soon as Laura conveyed the news. 'If she's on her way back I'll see the car and let you know. Go on up to her house and wait there.' He knew that Laura had a key, just as Rose did to Laura's house.

Jack flung himself into his car. What's the rush? he kept asking himself, it can't change anything. Nevertheless he drove faster than was safe and was relieved to see Rose's Metro parked neatly a few yards from Doreen's bungalow.

'Where could she be?' he asked a startled Doreen after he'd hammered on her door. Doreen shrugged. 'That woman could be anywhere.' She squinted down the road. 'Unless she's gone to see Nathan.'

Nathan. The man whose mother had died. Yes, that was it. Rose would not forget someone who was lonely.

'That house, the one with the mower outside.'

Jack walked quickly in the direction in which Doreen had pointed. There was no sign of life. The curtains in the front were half drawn and the rest of the window concealed by net. He rapped on the door. There was no answer. He knocked harder. 'Rose?' he shouted through the letter-box, feeling foolish as he did so. There was still no answer.

Jack turned the handle. Thank you, he whispered when the door opened. 'Rose?' he called louder. There was a noise from behind the door on his right. He pushed it open and stood, staring, at the scene in front of him. Bile rose in his throat. 'You filthy bastard,' he shouted as he raced towards Nathan Brown who stood with his trousers undone.

'Jack. No.' Rose's voice was no more than a croak but it was loud enough to remind him of his position.

She struggled upright, pulling her torn clothes around her. Her face was bruised where he'd hit her and her legs ached from where he'd tried to pull them apart. Never, ever had she been so glad to see Inspector Jack Pearce.

Jack's eyes did not leave Nathan Brown's face as he zipped up his trousers. He slumped into a chair and put his head in his hands. 'It was me,' he said, knowing that he had just forfeited his future, a future which, if he was honest, he may not have been able to cope with. 'Those girls. It was me.'

Jack reached into his pocket and pulled out his

phone. He issued a few short, sharp instructions then turned to Rose. Nathan was going nowhere, the man was defeated. 'Are you all right?' He hadn't meant to sound brusque but he didn't want to hear the answer.

She nodded. 'He didn't, he didn't,' but she couldn't complete the sentence.

'I couldn't. She's too old.' Nathan said innocently, looking up. It was then that Jack hit him. No police officer should act in that way, no matter how provoked, but it was too late to undo the deed.

Rose got to her feet. Her whole body was shaking. She staggered to where her phone lay on the floor and picked it up, steadying herself with one hand against the wall. 'I've got a message,' she managed to say. But before she could listen to it, Jack snatched the phone from her. He knew she was on automatic pilot, that no one in her circumstances could possibly be interested in a missed telephone call but he could not allow her to hear this one. 'It can wait.'

It was not long before several police officers arrived and took Nathan Brown away. Jack took Rose's arm and led her out to his car. 'I won't be a minute,' he told her once he had lowered her into the passenger seat. 'We need to get you to hospital but it can wait a minute or two.'

He walked a few yards away from the car and spoke to Laura, asking her to let everyone know that he was with Rose and that he would be in touch as soon as possible.

'What's happened, Jack?' Laura sensed immediately that all was not well.

He gave her a brief explanation after she had sworn to tell no one. 'That's why I can't tell her yet. Maybe in an hour or so.' Jack went back to the car.

'I'm not going to hospital. I want a bath.'

'It's evidence, Rose,' he said gently. He wanted to hold her, to stroke her hair and promise to make everything all right, but it was a promise he couldn't keep. He needed to be professional, to act as he would if this was another woman, one he didn't love.

'You'll have your evidence. He's raped two girls, DNA testing will prove that. He didn't rape me. The bruises will be evidence enough but I doubt that you'll need it. Take me home, please, Jack.'

He did so, driving very slowly and very carefully, aware of Doreen Clarke's plump frame behind her gate as he pulled away from the kerb.

'Someone can pick up your car tomorrow.' Rose didn't answer. She took her phone from her bag and depressed a button. 'Jack,' she said, 'why aren't you angry?' At other times when she had behaved stupidly he had been furious. She was staring at the displayed number of the missed call. 'Please tell me.'

'Not now.' He stared at the road refusing to look at her face.

'Why were you there at all? No one knew where I was going? What's going on here?' It was a puzzle but she didn't really care. All she wanted was to get home and run a bath and try to pretend it hadn't happened. She had not been raped, Lucy Chandler had been, and so had Nichola Rolland. Compared with them she was lucky, so how on earth must they have felt?

'Leave it for now, Rose. I promise I'll tell you when we get you home.'

Home. So he wasn't going to insist she went to hospital.

Laura was waiting anxiously at the house. She opened the door as soon as she heard his car in the drive. Sitting beside him was Rose, pale-faced beneath her tan. Laura couldn't imagine what the news would do to her at such a time. Jack went around to help Rose out then half carried her into the kitchen. 'Make some tea,' he told Laura.

Laura filled the kettle. For the first time in all the long years of their friendship she had no idea what to say to her friend.

Neither of them noticed Rose press the button to dial the number of the call she had missed until it was nearly too late. 'No. Don't do that.' Jack snatched the phone from her hand.

Rose shook from head to foot. 'It's my parents' number. Tell me what's wrong, Jack.'

He studied her face and felt his stomach sink. How could he cause more pain after her ordeal? But he had to. 'You father's been trying to reach you since about three o'clock this afternoon. He guessed you'd be out working but when he still couldn't get you at tea time he called Laura.'

'He'd lost your mobile phone number, Rose,' Laura added. 'I gave it to him then rang Jack and Barry then we both tried to find out where you were. Doreen said you'd been there and then Jack found you.'

Rose looked from one to the other. No, she thought. No. Don't let it be true. 'It's Mum, isn't it?'

Jack nodded. 'I'm so sorry,' he said as he reached for her hand. 'There was nothing anyone could do.'

'I wanted to go up, Dad said not to.'

Jack closed his eyes. It would all come, the guilt, the disbelief, the pain and the grief. But how much worse for Arthur Forbes?

'Who's with Dad?'

'June Potter.'

Rose stood up. 'I have to go to him.'

'Yes.' Jack knew it would be pointless to argue but she was not in a fit state to drive. 'Drink your tea first. Laura, can you put a shot of brandy in it?'

Laura went to find it. She touched Rose's shoulder as she walked past her chair.

'I need to make a phone call.' Jack, too, left the room. He rang the station where Nathan Brown would have been taken. Someone else would be dealing with the fall-out. For now Rose needed him. He explained he could be reached on his mobile if necessary and that a witness's mother had just died.

Rose was silent and dry-eyed throughout the whole of the journey. Jack concentrated on driving. Only when he pulled in to a service station did Rose turn to face him. 'Do we have to stop?'

'Yes. I need fuel and we both need coffee.' He did not add that another fifteen minutes or so would make no difference. Laura had rung Arthur to say they were on their way.

Rose had not wanted to speak to him. 'Face to face, not on the phone,' was all she had said when Laura tried to hand her Jack's mobile from which she had made the call.

And then they were pulling up outside the Cotswold cottage alongside the low, stone wall which sheltered the beautiful garden her parents had created. Arthur staggered out through the front door and reached for his daughter. 'I had a feeling, all along I had a feeling,' he said as he held Rose in his arms and stroked her hair. Only then did she cry. Sobs tore from her as she bent double as if she was in pain, loud noisy sobs which she couldn't contain. Both men watched her. There was nothing they could do, nothing they could say. Arthur's eyes were full of tears but he brushed them away with the back of his hand. Jack turned away and bit his lip as he, too, suddenly realised he would never see Evelyn Forbes again.

Finally they went into the house. June Potter was red-eyed but greeted them warmly. 'I'll go now,' she said. 'Just tell me when you want me to come back.'

'Thank you. I appreciate what you've done

for us.' Arthur got out a bottle of Glenmorangie and filled three tumblers. 'To Evelyn,' he said as he raised his own. 'To the best wife a man ever had.' He faced them each in turn. 'You've hurt yourself, Rose.'

'I fell,' she said, and left it at that.

Later that night when Arthur and Rose had gone to their rooms although probably not to sleep, Jack rang a sergeant on duty and discovered that Nathan Brown had made a full confession and that he had been charged with the murder of Nichola Rolland. Rose had suspected him, he realised that now, but she hadn't the sense to tell him so. How he wished she would confide in him more, how he wished he could live with her and take her pain away. But wishing for the impossible was a waste of time. Instead he would concentrate on the practicalities and try to get them through the days until the funeral. There would be no inquest, no post mortem, none of the added unpleasantness Nichola Rolland's parents had had to go through because Evelyn had been receiving current medical treatment, but that wouldn't make it any easier. He took the glasses out to the kitchen and washed and dried them. Tomorrow he would ensure they all ate but the Glenmorangie had been a good idea. Alcohol, in certain circumstances, was not a bad thing. It had loosened their tongues and allowed them to speak of Evelyn and remember things from the past.

He checked the fridge and cupboards. June Potter had obviously shopped; there was enough to keep them going for several days. No one had told him where he could sleep, so he lay on the comfortable chintz settee and closed his eyes. He thought about Rose and hoped that what she was feeling now would cancel out the earlier events of the day.

CHAPTER FIFTEEN

The summer was almost over. The sweltering heat of July and August when tarmac melted in the roads and stuck to the soles of shoes and ice-creams dripped over the back of hands unless they were eaten quickly had been replaced by a balmy September. Then, as often happened, the decent weather returned once the schools had gone back and most of the tourists had disappeared up the motorways. In the last week of September an Indian summer arrived with skies so blue they seemed unreal.

Rose sat next to her father on her garden bench. The yellowed grass was dry and scratchy beneath their feet and gave off a hay-like scent.

They sat quietly, enjoying the view. Closer now than they had ever been, there was no need for words.

Evelyn's funeral had taken place the week after she died. Rose had been surprised at the number of mourners. Tony Boyd had been there but seeing the proprietorial way in which Jack Pearce treated Rose and Arthur he understood the relationship. 'I meant to phone,' he told Rose in a quiet moment after the service, '*but* I had a London exhibition and then, well, to be honest, when Evelyn died I had no idea what I'd say to you.'

Rose realised then that there wouldn't be a phone call but that the two of them would remain friends. She was grateful to Tony for that.

She had stayed on for a further fortnight, assuring Jack they would be all right. He had returned to work.

'What will you do, Dad?' Rose had asked the day before she was due to drive back to Newlyn. She could not bear to think of him alone in that house.

'Take some time to decide. I don't want to rush things and make a terrible mistake.'

'I'll ring you every day. If you need me, you know where I am.'

But even now he had not come to a decision. He could stay where he was, sell up and buy somewhere new or, as Rose kept trying to persuade him, he could come and live with her. He had come down for an extended stay but deep down they both sensed that this would never become a permanent arrangement. Arthur had already visited several local estate agents and studied the details they had given him of houses in the area.

'What happened the day your mother died? You never did tell me and I couldn't get a word out of Jack. You didn't fall, did you?'

Rose, amazed that he had taken in her injuries, let alone remembered them, started at the beginning and relayed all of the events of those few weeks.

'Rape and murder. My God.' He did not comment on the danger Rose had been in because he had guessed it was the reason he had been left in the dark. 'And friends of yours involved, too.'

'It's all settled down now. Dave and Eva are about to move into their barn conversion although it isn't really fit to live in yet and Daphne and Rod are making a go of it. No one seems to have found out about his past after all.'

'I like Daphne, she's what they call a good

sort. And she seems happy enough working for Barry.' Arthur had been introduced to her in the shop.

Rose smiled. 'Yes. Barry.'

'Well, he's certainly made some improvements to that flat of his. It's like a different place. So light and airy and no doubt thanks to you.'

'No. It was his decision, he chose everything, I just went with him to buy the furniture. And you'll never guess.'

'No, not if you're involved, I won't. Tell me.'

'Back in July he went to some sort of do at Daphne's place and he met some new people. And . . .'

Arthur turned to her with surprise. 'You're not going to tell me he's got himself involved with a woman?'

'Got it in one. Well, not involved, exactly, but he takes her out every so often. She's divorced with one grown up daughter and I think they just enjoy one another's company.'

'Good heavens.' Arthur lit one of the cigars he had taken to smoking. 'They keep the midges away,' he had told Rose when she first commented on it. 'What about all the other people?'

'Samantha Jago's back at school and has stopped giving her mother a hard time. Joyce, by the way, is becoming a better and better artist. I hope she comes back when the term starts again.

'According to Laura, Lucy Chandler's changed. She's much quieter than she used to be and she's thinking of moving away when she's finished her hairdressing apprenticeship. I'm afraid she'll bear the scars for ever. Her mother also told Laura that she's lost interest in boys. She goes out with friends but gets a taxi home by herself. It hasn't made any difference that they caught Nathan.'

'From what Jack told me it seems you caught him single-handed.'

'It looks that way now, but I was going to tell Jack that very day.' Rose paused. It was a day and date she would never forget. 'And poor Doreen, she still feels partly responsible.'

'How come?'

'Because she tried to be a friend to Nathan and entertained him at the bungalow. On one occasion Nichola Rolland was passing and Doreen spoke to her. You know how Doreen likes to gossip, well she told Nathan that the girl was a loner and that she took herself off for long walks in the dunes to avoid the daily visits of an aunt who her mother had asked to keep an eye on her. Nathan took this in and followed her.'

'What about the other two?'

'Chance meetings, so Jack says. He was walking up to the garage when he saw Helen Trehearne turn off the road with her dog. She was otherwise alone so he simply took the opportunity. Lucy Chandler was a different matter. She was out with Jason and they'd had a row. It still isn't certain whether she was asked to act as a look-out for him and that's why they argued, but no one will ever know now. Anyway, Nathan had been over to Madron delivering some of his mother's things to one of her friends. He stayed for supper and was driving home when he saw her. He parked the car and went after her.'

'But why? I mean why now?'

Rose shrugged. 'Probably his mother's death released something in him. She stifled him, wouldn't allow him to mix with women. He was frustrated and he was known to be a mother's boy, he stood little chance with anyone local.' Rose felt the colour rise in her face as she recalled him saying she was too old. 'I think he couldn't cope with people his own age and he probably wanted to dominate as he'd been dominated. Home-spun psychology, but that's my theory.' She did not add that her suspicions had been aroused by reading a novel, a novel in which a domineering mother had finally driven her son too far and he'd killed her. Nathan had not killed his mother but with her death something inside him had snapped and he had had no idea how to handle his newfound freedom. Before he had had time to adjust to his new situation all his repressed desires had risen to the surface. Nor did she mention that she had guessed the acquisition of the video had been to enable him to watch pornographic material. Several tapes had been found in his possession when the police searched the house.

'Now, don't you think it's time we got ready?' Rose got up to take in their coffee mugs. It was still warm but the sun moved around lower in the sky now. Another few weeks and they would gain an hour on the clock but darkness would come earlier and earlier.

'You carry on, love, it won't take me long. I'll just sit here and enjoy the warmth and the view for a few more moments.'

Rose kissed the top of his head where his hair was thinning. He looks older, she realised and he's lost weight. But otherwise he looked reasonably well.

Upstairs she showered and washed her hair then, in her underclothes, put on her make-up as she decided what to wear. It would be colder later on. The tan skirt with a silk vest top a shade lighter would be ideal as there was a long cardigan jacket to match the skirt. She sprayed perfume into the air and walked into the vapour as Laura had recently told her this was the correct thing to do. Ready to go, she went downstairs and waited for her father to emerge from the spare room and the taxi to arrive to take them to the Mount's Bay Inn where they were meeting Jack. He was treating them to a meal and had suggested that Laura and Trevor came too, or Barry if Arthur preferred.

'Thanks, Jack, but I'm not up to facing more than one or two people at a time yet. Another time, maybe.'

So it was to be just the three of them.

The taxi arrived on time and dropped them outside the pub on the seafront. Jack was at the bar looking very handsome in well cut trousers, and a shirt and jacket. He smiled, genuinely pleased to see them and gave Rose an appreciative wink.

'We'll sit in the window,' Rose said in deference to her father who had walked quite a long way that day. They had driven around the coastline then walked part of the way along the coastal path, stopping at a small cafe with outside tables where they had sipped China tea and eaten home made scones with butter and strawberry jam and dollops of thick, crusty clotted cream. The fire, to the left of the counter, had been lit in its burner and was throwing out more heat than was necessary this early in the evening which was another reason for moving away from the bar.

They had one drink before walking down to the Seafarer's restaurant where Rose was supposed to have gone with Jack back at the end of June. It was just off the Promenade. Downstairs was the bar area, the dining tables were on the first floor. Situated on a corner and with large windows on two sides, there was a view of the bay wherever you sat.

Elizabet and Romano greeted them warmly as they were shown to their seats. The meal would be lengthy, Romano cooked everything from scratch and choosing from the menu was not an easy task either, not with fish specialities as well as game and goose and pasta and steaks. Elizabet brought them olives and home-made bread and Jack ordered the wine.

'I've told Dad about Nathan,' Rose said in case Jack was worried about mentioning the subject.

'It seems as if my daughter's been detecting

again,' Arthur said with a smile to show he wasn't denigrating Jack's efforts.

'No one seems able to stop her, hard as we try Have you made any plans yet, Arthur?'

'No, but I'm sure my head'll clear in another couple of weeks.'

'You mean you'll know if you can stand living in the house of a mad woman by then?'

'Quite.' Arthur lifted the cloth covering the warm bread and reached for the garlic butter. He had seen the flush in his daughter's face and knew Jack was on dangerous ground. If only Rose would marry him one decision would definitely be taken out of his hands. He would not dream of moving in if Jack was there on a permanent basis. In fact, he really already knew he would not be moving in. What he wanted was to find a home nearby. That way he could see Rose often but they would both retain their independence. There was no way he could stay where he was, there were far too many memories of Evelyn and the work they had both put into the garden.

They ate and drank and tasted each other's food, all of which was exceptionally good, and they talked of Rose and Jack's friends. It was Evelyn's name that wasn't mentioned until almost the end of the evening. 'I keep trying to think what she'd have wanted me to do, or what she'd have done if the situation was reversed. I know it's daft, that the short time I have left is my own, but she's still with me, you see. She always will be.'

'There's no rush,' Jack said quickly, noticing Rose's sad expression. 'I mean, look at the two of us. Rose goes on all the time about getting married but I like my freedom too much. Give me five years or so and I might consider her offer.'

Rose was staring at him in amazement. He was poker-faced until a smile twitched at the corner of his lips. 'Oh, honestly, Jack,' she said with a laugh as she indicated that her glass was empty.

'You can fill mine up, too then we'll order another bottle. I'll foot the drinks bill,' Arthur said.

Rose listened as the two men she loved most in the world began a discussion on politics. He can still hold an intellectual conversation, she thought, admiring her father's continuing interest and his ability to do so so soon after her mother's death. He's far better at coping than I was when David died. But maybe age does that to you, maybe you come to accept the idea before it happened. And life did go on. Look at me now, she thought, successful and actually making money from my painting and another local exhibition at Christmas to work towards. But life hadn't gone on for Nichola Rolland and it had changed completely for Lucy Chandler. Rose knew she was lucky, that she would bear no scars from her encounter with Nathan Brown because of the events which had overtaken it.

'You're smiling,' Jack commented.

'Yes. I was thinking of all the things we've got planned for the next couple of weeks. We'll be exhausted.' Each and every one of her friends had invited her and her father for drinks or a meal or, in Barry's case, a day out in Falmouth or Truro or Plymouth or anywhere else they wanted to go.

'And she'll do some work in between,' Arthur said sternly, 'or I'll put her across my knee.'

'You're a braver man than I am even to suggest it.'

Arthur met his eyes and smiled, really smiled, for the first time for months. You'll do, Jack Pearce, he thought, you'll more than do. It's just such a bloody shame my stubborn daughter can't see it.

If you enjoyed *Killed in Cornwall*,
read on to find out about more books
by Janie Bolitho . . .

BURIED IN CORNWALL

Rose Trevelyan lives peacefully in Cornwall after the death of her husband, working as an artist and photographer. But when she hears terrified screams as she paints the rugged Cornish countryside, and a local woman is reported missing, Rose finds herself suddenly caught at the centre of a police investigation.

With so many people who trust her, Rose is – reluctantly, at times – privy to the secrets of many. When the things she is told in confidence appear connected to the investigation, Rose must decide how far the bonds of friendship reach.